TARGET EIGHT

(THE SPY GAME–BOOK 8)

JACK MARS

Jack Mars

Jack Mars is the USA Today bestselling author of the LUKE STONE thriller series, which includes seven books. He is also the author of the new FORGING OF LUKE STONE prequel series, comprising six books; of the AGENT ZERO spy thriller series, comprising twelve books; of the TROY STARK thriller series, comprising seven books; of the SPY GAME thriller series, comprising ten books; of the JAKE MERCER thriller series, comprising five books (and counting); and of the new TYLER WOLF thriller series, comprising five books (and counting).

Jack loves to hear from you, so please feel free to visit www.Jackmarsauthor.com to join the email list, receive a free book, receive free giveaways, connect on Facebook and Twitter, and stay in touch!

ISBN: 978-1-0943-8467-2

BOOKS BY JACK MARS

TYLER WOLF THRILLER SERIES
DOUBLE AGENT (Book #1)
DOUBLE CROSS (Book #2)
DOUBLE ASSET (Book #3)
DOUBLE DOCTRINE (Book #4)
DOUBLE JEOPARDY (Book #5)

JAKE MERCER THRILLER SERIES
ABSOLUTE THREAT (Book #1)
ABSOLUTE DAMAGE (Book #2)
ABSOLUTE FORCE (Book #3)
ABSOLUTE PERIL (Book #4)
ABSOLUTE TREASON (Book #5)

THE SPY GAME
TARGET ONE (Book #1)
TARGET TWO (Book #2)
TARGET THREE (Book #3)
TARGET FOUR (Book #4)
TARGET FIVE (Book #5)
TARGET SIX (Book #6)
TARGET SEVEN (Book #7)
TARGET EIGHT (Book #8)
TARGET NINE (Book #9)
TARGET TEN (Book #10)

TROY STARK THRILLER SERIES
ROGUE FORCE (Book #1)
ROGUE COMMAND (Book #2)
ROGUE TARGET (Book #3)
ROGUE MISSION (Book #4)
ROGUE SHOT (Book #5)
ROGUE STRIKE (Book #6)
ROGUE ORDER (Book #7)

LUKE STONE THRILLER SERIES
ANY MEANS NECESSARY (Book #1)

OATH OF OFFICE (Book #2)
SITUATION ROOM (Book #3)
OPPOSE ANY FOE (Book #4)
PRESIDENT ELECT (Book #5)
OUR SACRED HONOR (Book #6)
HOUSE DIVIDED (Book #7)

FORGING OF LUKE STONE PREQUEL SERIES
PRIMARY TARGET (Book #1)
PRIMARY COMMAND (Book #2)
PRIMARY THREAT (Book #3)
PRIMARY GLORY (Book #4)
PRIMARY VALOR (Book #5)
PRIMARY DUTY (Book #6)

AN AGENT ZERO SPY THRILLER SERIES
AGENT ZERO (Book #1)
TARGET ZERO (Book #2)
HUNTING ZERO (Book #3)
TRAPPING ZERO (Book #4)
FILE ZERO (Book #5)
RECALL ZERO (Book #6)
ASSASSIN ZERO (Book #7)
DECOY ZERO (Book #8)
CHASING ZERO (Book #9)
VENGEANCE ZERO (Book #10)
ZERO ZERO (Book #11)
ABSOLUTE ZERO (Book #12)

PROLOGUE

Harper Canyon Dam
Northern Nevada
10 a.m.

Yongju Choi felt a spring in his step as he made his rounds in the bowels of the giant hydroelectric dam. This was his first day as chief engineer, and at only thirty-two he was the youngest chief engineer of a hydroelectric dam in all of the United States.

His parents over in Phoenix had been ecstatic when he got promoted, as had been his fiancée. They were to be married in a month. What perfect timing! She wanted to have a child right away, and his pay raise meant that it would be no problem.

The only problem was that they lived in the middle of nowhere. Harper Canyon had a medium-sized river going through a narrow gorge, which had made it ideal for the engineers back in the late Sixties to dam it for electricity. The power had to be shipped pretty far to get the any big cities, but at least there hadn't been many local landowners to pay off. The only locals lived in the town of Pay Dirt ten miles downstream, population 10,000.

A hick town. It was bigger in the 1860s during the local gold rush than it was now. These days it relied on tourism centered around a hokey Western town, the occasional movie shoot, and a bit of light industry. He was the only Korean-American in the whole county. That made people stare. They stared more when they saw him with Wendy, a six-foot blonde Texan. They weren't nasty stares, just kind of "where did you come from" stares. Still, it was pretty annoying.

He shouldn't complain, Yongju Choi thought as he checked the flow levels through the penstock leading to the turbines. They were within tolerable limits. No need to widen or narrow the entrance. The turbines were working at top capacity too. Everything was fine.

Including his life. So what if Pay Dirt's idea of cosmopolitanism was ordering extra hot sauce at Taco Bell? Sure, he was a long way from his hometown of San Francisco, but he had a great job, and housing prices were cheap.

Yongju Choi finished his checks and moved on to the filter monitors. As the great torrent of water moved through the dam, a large steel mesh kept logs and other debris from getting into the turbines. While the huge steel drums that spun to create electricity could withstand a lot of force, replacing them would cost millions so a screen of thick steel bars like in a prison kept the largest objects from getting through. Sensitive monitors measured the speed of flow just before and just after the screen in order to tell how much of the flow was being blocked by debris. When it got too much, each of the channels through the dam would be shut off in turn, and a crew would go down with chainsaws to cut up any logs and clean everything out.

Flow levels were just fine. He moved on to the engineering office and asked for Fred Garrick, one of the engineers. The guy was a relatively new hire and hadn't given him his daily report like he should have. While Garrick came with good references, Choi found the guy a bit spacey, like his mind wasn't totally on his work.

In the office he found Mindy Nolen, another of the engineers, tapping away at a computer. No one else was around.

"Hey Mindy, you seen Fred?"

"He was feeling sick and went home."

"Oh, when?" *Nice if he had told me.*

"About half an hour ago."

Choi resisted the urge to say what he thought. He hated inefficiency. He had a good team here, but Garrick was turning out to be the weakest link.

"Did he file a report on the extermination crew?"

A crew of exterminators had come in for the last couple of days to clear out the rats and cockroaches that got attracted by the moisture and human activity of this place. They had spent much of their time at the deepest levels of dam, a couple of levels below where Choi and Nolen now stood, where a pair of large rooms apparently had nests of rats. They'd taken ages. Choi had assumed they'd come in spray the whole place, and be gone in a couple of hours.

"Um, I don't know," Mindy said.

"Are they gone now too?"

"Yes, they left an hour ago."

Choi decided to go down to the bottom level and see for himself. He took the stairs two flights down, tried to open the steel door, and found it locked.

"What the hell?"

Grumbling, he fished out his mass of keys, found the right one, and put it in the lock.

Or tried to. He couldn't get it more than a third of the way in.

"What the hell?" he repeated.

He crouched and turned on the little flashlight he had for a keychain.

Peering into the lock, he could see a bit of metal jammed inside. It looked like the broken-off end of a paperclip.

A strange feeling went over him, a cold prickling like a grim premonition.

Something's wrong. Something's very wrong.

Choi tried to tell himself that he was overreacting, that there was a perfectly valid reason why Fred had left early without telling him he had screwed up the lock to the lower level.

Because it had to have been him. He was the only one who had come down here. He had been escorting the exterminators, and that was the only reason anyone had come down to the lowest level today.

But why would he break off a piece of paperclip in the lock? That made no sense.

Unless he did it deliberately to keep anyone from getting inside.

Once again, a gut fear overcame his reasoning. Choi tried to calm himself.

Tried and failed.

Alarm bells rang in his head, alarm bells he couldn't explain and couldn't ignore.

He ran up the stairs, taking them two at a time, and found a couple of the maintenance guys. Choi told them the problem, and they stared at him with amusement that soon grew into concern.

"Why would he jam the lock?" one of the crew asked.

"No idea. Can you fix it?"

They grabbed toolboxes and went down to the door. The maintenance guys studied the lock, hemmed and hawed, then shook their heads.

"No way to get that out. We're going to have to drill the lock out and replace it."

"What's going on here?" Choi demanded.

They could only shrug.

It was a matter of minutes to set up the drill, drill through the lock, and pull it out. After that, they could manually flip the lock and open the door. The room beyond was dark. Feeling a bit timid, Yongju Choi stepped inside, groped for the light switches, and flipped them on.

Harsh florescent lights buzzed on one by one. The chief engineer and the two maintenance men moved through the room, examining the machinery and finding it all in place.

That is, until they rounded the bank of machinery and came to the far wall.

There they stopped dead and stared.

At regular intervals along the floor, holes had been drilled into the concrete and filled with shaped charges. Choi recognized them from work he had done with a mining company a couple of years before. A thick insulated wire ran like an anaconda between them, ending at a small box with a couple of lights and a timer.

Choi and his two employees never got to see how much time was left on it, because at that moment the time ran out.

The blast disintegrated them instantly and shook the entire structure. Two floors up, Mindy Nolen was thrown to the floor. A second later, the shockwave tore up the stairs, blowing an intervening door off its hinges before hitting Mindy's level. She was thrown against the wall and killed instantly, along with everyone else on that level.

Those on the upper levels were injured, some knocked unconscious, others left in a daze, wondering what had just happened.

They never got the time to figure that out.

The shuddering of the dam didn't cease. It only grew stronger. The blast had created deep cracks in the structure below the waterline. Concrete crumbled, the steel rebars groaned and bent, and then in a terrible detonation heard miles away, the dam shattered, the immense weight of water behind it breaking it into countless pieces.

Millions of square feet of water rushed down Harper Canyon like a tsunami.

It took out a bridge a few miles down the canyon, snapping the concrete structure like a twig and plunging the cars into the swirl of water and debris.

The flow continued, carrying pieces of the dam and bridge with it to slam into curves of the canyon, shearing off more rocks until it reached the town of Pay Dirt, population 10,000.

Wendy, Yongju Choi's wife, was completely unaware of what happened as she sat in her sculpture studio working on a marble statue for a client, earbuds in her ears playing loud classic rock.

She felt the initial rumble as the dam broke and her husband died, but she dismissed that as a truck passing outside.

The second vibration of the approaching flood made her curious. Were they doing some construction on her street?

She set aside her mallet and chisel, stood, and reached to take out her earbuds.

Just then the water hit Pay Dirt, and the Choi household and every other building in town was swept away.

Every single person in Pay Dirt died within seconds.

CHAPTER ONE

Rural Virginia
That same day

Jana Peters relaxed in a lounge chair reading the latest issue of the *Journal of Roman Archaeology* while the heady aroma of grilling venison filled her nostrils.

It had been three months since they had wiped out Dr. Moswen Farag and his terrorist team from The Sword of the Righteous and she and Jacob Snow were enjoying a well-earned holiday on a CIA expense account. The CIA had put them up in a cabin in a wooded area of rural Virginia and had given them fresh IDs. All their wounds had healed, and they had settled into a quiet routine. Jacob went out bow hunting almost every day and Jana was reading to her heart's content.

She had asked for a leave of absence from her university, citing health problems. They had been quick to agree. She could go back to her old career anytime she wanted to.

Jana looked around the cozy interior of the cabin with its Navajo rugs on the floor and hunting trophies on the walls. The CIA really knew how to lay out some hospitality when it wasn't taking out terrorists. They had fifty acres of woodland that kept them out of sight of the nearest neighbors and cover stories to explain why neither of them had a visible source of income. All they had to do was relax, heal, and enjoy each other's company.

"Jana, can you come here and open the wine?" Jacob called from the kitchen.

"All right."

She put her bookmark into the journal, set it aside, and stood. A bit of red wine would go well with the venison, not that she needed it. If she got any more relaxed, she felt her heart might stop.

That was becoming a problem. Jana had never been used to inactivity, and there was only so much reading and hiking you could do before you wanted something more substantive. She missed lecturing, she missed working in the lab, and she really missed planning and directing excavations in the field.

And she never thought she'd feel this, but she also missed going on missions.

Jana entered their spacious and well-appointed kitchen to find Jacob, all healed up from the battering of the last few missions, tending the steaks on the grill.

"The wine's over there. Sorry I couldn't open it myself but the venison is almost done and it's so easy to overcook. I made a blackberry sauce to go with it."

He gestured to a pan on a stove element set to low. Jana's mouth watered. She had not expected Jacob Snow to turn out to be a good cook. Another of his many talents, although his cooking was mainly limited to meat. In a spare room, he had set up a home brewery kit and was experimenting with making beer. In another room, he was making furniture. So far those projects hadn't been as successful as his cooking.

"Is this the one you bagged yesterday?" she asked as she fetched the corkscrew and set to work on the bottle, a fine Rioja from Spain.

"Yeah. Fresh out of the forest. I named him Bambi before I shot him."

"Very funny."

He looked at her with mock surprise. "You're not shocked? Your delicate sensibilities haven't been scandalized?"

"You're going to have to do a lot better than that," she said, pulling out the cork with a satisfying pop.

"And here we go." Jacob presented the two plates adorned with medium rare venison steaks, blackberry sauce, and green beans with herbal butter melting on top of them.

Jana smiled. "Delicious. Let's eat."

They sat at a little table in the conservatory, a glass-enclosed annex where they could see trees all around them. Squirrels scampered up and down a couple of the oaks. A hummingbird hovered around a feeder just outside, a flash of blue on the background greens and browns.

The venison was rich and tender, perfectly cooked.

"Mmm. Bambi didn't die in vain," Jana said.

"Yeah," Jacob replied, looking out at the beautiful view before his eyes settled on her. "I can get used to this."

"You're not bored?" She'd been worried about that. He'd lived such an active life, and now he was basically living like a retired man twice his age. Except for the bow hunting, although Jana could imagine him still doing that in his sixties.

He leaned over the table and punctuated his answer with a series of kisses. “Not. At. All.”

"Good. I'm finding it a bit quiet, but it's a good quiet. I think we've earned it."

“Totally. Maybe we can make a permanent thing out of it.”

Jana smiled and tucked into her meal. Of course, this wouldn't be permanent. This was more like a sabbatical.

Wait. Was that what he was referring to?

She looked up at Jacob. He was studying her, wine glass in hand, with an expression she’d never seen in him before.

“What kind of permanent thing?”

Jacob gave an exaggerated shrug and hid himself behind his wine glass.

“Well, if you’re talking about you cooking lunch permanently, then feel free to hunt down some more venison.”

“You might get bored with it after twenty or thirty years, but we can always move to Canada where I can hunt elk.”

“Maybe I’ll get bored with the cook instead,” Jana teased.

"Oh, I think we're past that stage. You hated me for a while, but that was only because you couldn't accept the fact that I'm irresistible."

“Suuuure.”

Jacob raised his glass. “To Bambi, and to all the elk we’ll eat in Canada ten years from now.”

Jana’s heart performed a somersault. This joking was getting a little too specific, and it wasn’t the first time one of them had brought it up. It thrilled her and scared her a bit too.

Then she realized that being scared was a ridiculous reaction. She was with the man she loved, the man she had saved the world with several times over. Would settling down be such a bad idea?

“You got your workout today?” Jacob asked. When one of them steered too close to talk of permanence, they'd always pull back with talk of something completely unrelated.

“Yeah. I’ll leave right after I wash up here. I’ll pick up something for dinner when I’m in town.”

“Don’t faceplant on the treadmill again, all right?” Jacob said.

They both laughed. “I needed an injury to remind myself of the good old days.”

"Good? Not so sure about that. Well, I'll take you getting a split lip over a gunshot wound any day."

"Ditto."

A flash of green outside the window made them both look. A pair of hummingbirds, one blue and one green, danced around each other in the air.

They watched in silence for a time. Jacob reached over and put his hand over hers, where it rested on the table. Their fingers interlaced, but they said nothing as the two beautiful creatures continued their mating ritual.

***

Jacob looked over his plate at the woman of his dreams and felt a growing sense of unease. It all seemed so perfect, and he had been around the block too many times to think that something perfect could endure. He dreaded the phone, dreaded email. Sooner or later, the world would come crashing in and disrupt this wonderful indolence.

He had done nothing the past few months. Sure, he had worked out, built a tool shed, hunted deer, and learned basic woodworking, fooled around with brewing, but he hadn't heard a shot fired in anger in three months. He hadn't even been to the gunnery range for the better part of a month.

And he loved every moment of it—the smell of wood smoke in the early dawn, the birdsong as he and Jana did their morning jog along forest trails, the easy lovemaking, the intimate dinners. Jana was a wonderful companion. He wanted this to last forever.

But the world was what the world was. It would not last forever. Tyler Wallace had been a good man and hadn't called him in for anything, not even any intel analysis. When he had ordered Jacob to take a break, he had actually meant it.

It couldn't last. Not looking at the Internet or switching on the TV would not shut out the world forever. One day, or maybe five minutes from now, his encrypted satellite phone would ring and he'd have to answer the call to duty.

And then what? Another mission where he'd have to gun down a bunch of people he'd never met? Another saving the world type scenario that left thousands of innocent people dead and himself and the woman he loved psychologically scarred?

No. He didn't want to go through that again. He *couldn't* go through that again.

Jacob Snow was on the cusp of doing something he had never once considered doing before.

Quitting the CIA.

He didn't know what he'd do if he quit, and he didn't care. He could always find something. Sooner or later, Jana would go back to teaching. With that and whatever he got on the side, plus the pension he was already eligible for, they'd be OK financially.

He'd been writing and rewriting his resignation letter in his head for a couple of weeks now and almost had it down. In it he praised his colleagues, especially Tyler Wallace and Aaron Peters, Jana's father, and saying how proud he was to have worked for such a fine organization while making it clear that this resignation was final and he did not want to discuss it further.

He hadn't typed a single word into the computer. Sitting down and opening a new .doc file felt like too much of a commitment.

He'd do it soon, though. Jacob felt that he'd do it really soon.

CHAPTER TWO

Aaron Peters was getting bored. He sat on the end of his private pier on an isolated lake in northern Maine, a fishing rod in his hand, eyes unfocused on the hypnotic ripple of the sea.

The CIA had done right by him, letting him have an unlimited leave to rest, recuperate, and get integrated back into normal society.

The rest and recuperation had taken a week. After that his batteries were charged and all the minor injuries he'd suffered in the last mission had healed.

Integrating back into civilian life wasn't proving so easy.

Every time he woke up in the morning, he wished he was in a tent on rocky ground. Every time he brewed his morning coffee, he wished it was over an open fire instead of in a modern kitchen. When he went fishing, he wished he could drop a grenade into the lake and get his fish the quick and easy way.

Civilian life was boring and unfulfilling, and he had told his bosses so. They had remained adamant, however.

"You've been out in the field longer than anyone we've ever had in the organization," Tyler Wallace had told him. "Sure, we got deep moles who've been on active duty for longer, but they spend most of their time living a false but mundane life. You were on active duty in the harshest regions in the world. You need time to heal, outside and inside."

Faultless logic. He still wasn't buying it. He wanted a mission, and he wanted it now. All this training and experience was going to waste. He felt useless, just another civilian slouching through life while the world fell to pieces.

Flanking him on the pier was an encrypted satellite phone, just in case they wanted to call him, and on the other side a sensitive shortwave radio tuned to China's Arabic overseas service. Always a good idea to listen to the propaganda of a rising superpower. You never knew what you might hear.

And what he heard almost made him drop his fishing rod straight into the lake.

"Initial reports from the United States say that a hydroelectric dam in the state of Nevada has burst," the announcer said in Arabic with a Chinese accent. "Police have not ruled out a terrorist attack. The dam, while more than fifty years old, has no record of fault or obvious decay. Witnesses tell of a deep boom that shook the dam and the land around it. Cracks appeared in the structure, and the dam burst within a matter of moments, sending water rushing down the river and washing away a town of an estimated 10,000 inhabitants. We will continue to bring updates of this developing story."

The announcer went on to talk about a Chinese-led road-building project in Pakistan. Aaron switched the radio off. He pulled out his cell phone—something he had never had much use for as he crept around the remotest parts of the world, and brought up CNN.

The images he saw splashed across the website left him stunned.

Aaron put away his cell phone and picked up his satellite phone, punching in the code that allowed the phone to function.

He needed to make a call to Tyler Wallace. His nation needed him again.

***

Jana drove into town, whistling happily to herself. She was off to her kickboxing class, the highlight of her week. While she loved her and Jacob's little love shack, it was getting dull. She had tasted the life of an international operative, and it had gotten under her skin.

Not that she missed the violence and killing—that had always disturbed her and always will—but she missed the jet setting, the problem solving, the *importance* of it all.

She missed making a difference.

But she understood Jacob needed a break. He'd been fighting too long, lost too much, and he needed to recuperate. Her father was doing the same up in Maine, and she hoped he was getting back into normal life.

Her life, though, needed to stay exciting. She couldn't stay home reading and making love all day.

Well, she thought with a smile. *Some days, I sure can.*

It certainly was helping Jacob. His whole demeanor had changed. He smiled more, didn't study his surroundings constantly, and was generally more at ease. The peace and quiet did him a world of good, and gave her a glimpse into what Jacob Snow might have been if he had lived a normal life.

Which is why she hadn't told him about the kickboxing class. Too close to his old job. Hell, he might even want to join, and that might lead to flashbacks. That's why, when her sparring partner got a punch through her guard and split her lip, she had made up a story of falling on the treadmill at the local gym.

She felt a bit bad about the fib, but Jacob needed his rest.

Jana pulled into the parking lot of her kickboxing gym, tucked away on a back street of the town in a concrete box of a building. As she entered through the heavy steel door she got hit with the smell of male sweat and socks. The stench was the scariest part. The guys—and they were all guys—had turned out to be pretty welcoming.

The interior of the kickboxing gym was a Spartan place. A rack of free weights stood to one side near a bare concrete floor where a couple of guys were skipping rope to get warmed up while others benched heavy loads. To the other side were a series of punching bags which guys kicked and punched, some with gloves, other bare knuckle.

Jana always wore gloves. She did a lot of typing in her job, and she didn't want to hurt her hands.

Her gaze was drawn to the main attraction of this smelly, windowless place—the ring at the center. Two guys were squaring off, hands gloved, feet and heads in padding, trading punches and kicks as they circled each other while a burly Samoan instructor, Iosefa Solaita, shouted out advice and encouragement to both fighters.

She walked up to the side of the ring.

"Hey, Iosefa, why don't you put me in cold?"

The man's barrel chest shook with mirth. "Glutton for punishment, eh?" OK, girl, you're in. Kirk, get the hell out of there. Mitch, stay in the ring and get ready for a real fight. Don't go easy on her because she's a girl."

"I won't," Mitch said.

Mitch was the guy who gave her the split lip. Six foot, square body of muscle and meat, unibrow shading perceptive blue eyes that always looked for an opening and usually found it. She had plans for him.

Jana shucked off her hoodie and sweatpants, put on pads, and stepped into the ring. A few of the other guys gathered around. There had been all the usual teasing when she first showed up here a couple of months before, but that vanished soon enough when the only woman in the gym started winning matches.

Not against Mitch, though. Not yet.

Even though Mitch was 2-0 with her, he stood in his corner watching her warily. Those two wins had both been close ones.

Jana got to her corner and limbered up. She had skipped the warmup and bag practice to go straight into the fight. She wanted to make it harder for herself.

"OK, fighters, show me your mouthpieces. I want a clean fight. Protect yourself at all times. Come to the center and touch gloves."

Mitch didn't hesitate to come forward and offer his gloved right hand for her to touch with her own. He always showed her respect before kicking her around the ring.

She thought she'd figured out Mitch's weakness, though. His kicks were flashy, but his big body made them a bit slow, and she noticed that he dropped his guard slightly on the recovery. That might give her an opening.

Now was the time to see if she was right.

If she was wrong, she was due for another ass kicking. She'd have to think up a different excuse if she came back with a bloody lip again this time.

They touched gloves and returned to their corners.

"Ready?" Iosefa Solaita asked. "You better be. Now get in there and let's see what you got!"

Jana wasn't as strong as Mitch, but she was faster. She darted in, landing a jab and missing with a cross before ducking back, Mitch's right hook missing her by less than an inch. Huh. He was getting faster. Must be because he was warmed up and she wasn't. A disadvantage. Good.

She darted in again, failed to get through Mitch's guard, and popped back out of range before he could counterattack.

Jana repeated the movement, but Mitch was ready for her this time and she blocked a killer cross that made her arms sing with pain. That was going to bruise. She'd have to make love to Jacob in the dark so he wouldn't see.

The two fighters circled, ducking and weaving, looking for openings.

Suddenly, Mitch lashed out with a kick. Jana ducked back, not wanting a taste of his stanky feet. She'd gotten that in the last fight, and it wasn't a pleasant experience.

He missed, and misinterpreted her retreat as fear. He followed up with a feint and another kick that she soaked up with a block.

And just like she thought, he recovered a bit too slowly and brought his guard down a bit too much.

Just enough for her to land a hard right cross square in his face.

It wasn't enough to take him down, especially not since she wore gloves and he wore face padding, but it did stun him for a moment. Jana gave him a thigh kick that off-balanced him further, then a one-two punch that landed squarely.

Mitch replied with a right hook of such power that Jana had no choice but to dodge. Her opponent held his ground, using that one second to regain his balance and bring up his guard.

When she went in again, he was ready for her. They traded punches, both landing although not solidly, and they circled again. Jana landed a couple of leg kicks to give him something to think about, and Mitch replied with a kick to her side that had her entire rib cage singing in chorus.

I shouldn't underestimate his kicks too much.

They circled, Jana landed a jab, dodged another kick, and tried to get in when his guard came down but he recovered too quickly.

Has he learned from his mistake?

Apparently not, because he tried to finish the fight early with a decapitating roundhouse. This man was true to his word and not "going easy on her because she's a girl."

But it turned out the stronger the kick (and it was horrifying) the longer the recovery. Jana darted in, gave him a left cross, followed by a thigh kick to keep him off balance a moment longer, then a right hook that sent him staggering.

Dimly, she was aware of cheering. Her focus kept it in the background and she swept in give Mitch some more punishment.

Of course, padded up as they were, she didn't get a knockout, but she chased him around the ring for the rest of the round, only getting a few jabs as the price for victory.

When their trainer called time, there was no doubt who had won the round. She looked out over the assembled crowd—all those tough guys—and found they weren't paying attention to the fight anymore.

They were all staring at the TV hanging in the far corner, which was usually tuned to ESPN. A breaking news story showed a dam somewhere in the United States had burst. The camera switched from a helicopter shot of the burst dam to an aerial view of some town, or at least what had been a town. Most of it had been swept away, only a few tops of buildings remaining visible. Bodies, debris, and vehicles floated in the muddy swirl.

The scrolling news ticker running along the bottom said, “Dept. of Homeland Security says Harper Canyon Dam disaster probably the work of a bomber.”

Oh, hell.

CHAPTER THREE

Two hours later, as she came out of the supermarket with a couple of bags of groceries, still stunned by the news from Nevada, Jana spotted something strange.

A Mercedes with tinted windows was parked next to her car, and an older gentleman stood beside it. He was tall, probably six-four, with a lanky build, a deeply tanned face from long hours in the sun, and salt and pepper hair swept back in a rather affected style. He wore a conservative tailored suit, the jacket of which hung a bit loosely on his frame.

When you see that, her father used to say, *it's a good sign that he's got a shoulder holster.*

Dad's advice kept turning out to be useful.

While that got her on alert, she did not feel any fear, only a heightened awareness. The stranger was looking right at her and making no attempt to be subtle about it, and while that closed car could hold other people, a quick glance around the parking lot didn't reveal anyone else who was obviously watching or following her.

"Ms. Peters," the man said in a cultured accent that spoke of Ivy League privilege, "how good to meet you."

"Can I help you?" Jana asked, giving him a wide berth and setting her grocery bags on the hood of her car.

"You don't know me, but my name is Robert Bradshaw, and I am a fellow archaeologist."

"Oh. What specialty?"

Archaeology was a small enough discipline that if someone did similar work to you, you were bound to know them at least by reputation.

"I do not specialize in any particular period or region. I'm a conservationist and … research coordinator."

The odd pause before that last statement made her wonder if it was entirely accurate.

"Which museum?"

"I'm the director of the Antiquities Division." Suspicion rose up in her. She'd never heard of that. Before she could formulate an answer, Mr. Bledshaw said, "I suppose you've never heard of us."

"No. It's a division of what?"

"The United States government. We aim to preserve and retrieve antiquities in danger of destruction."

Jana cocked her head. "So you're here because … "

Bledshaw gave an accommodating smile as if to apologize for beating around the bush. "While your accomplishments have been kept from the press, Dr. Peters, there is a small circle in government who have heard of them and are universal in their approval and respect. We think you'd make a fine addition to our organization."

"Are you CIA?" He didn't strike her as CIA. Too upper class. Too Ivy League.

"We have worked with that fine organization in the past and they have kept us informed of your movements." He chuckled. "I must admit there has been more than a little soul-searching in the Antiquities Division about the fact that you discovered and saved so many important artifacts that we missed."

"Did Tyler Wallace send you?"

"A fine gentleman. No. We are independent of the CIA, although we work with them from time to time."

Jana blinked. This was getting weird.

"I see," she said, although she didn't. "And why are you reaching out to me now?"

Because of Nevada? Dad always says he doesn't believe in coincidence.

"Because of your fine accomplishments, and because we see a window of opportunity. You are not working at the moment, and this is the perfect time to suggest a career change."

"To what?"

"To being on our conservation team. As your recent adventures have taught you, the world's archaeological heritage is far richer, and far more dangerous, than most scholars could ever imagine."

Jana stiffened. That was surely a reference to the Staves of Ra, a series of ancient staves that contained naturally occurring uranium 235, a rarity and the same isotope used in nuclear weapons. This fissile material was kept safe in a lead sheath and the radiation focused through a crude collimator. The Sword of the Righteous had tried more than once to obtain one of these staves in order to build a nuclear device and detonate it in the West.

In Rome a few months ago, they had come within a few seconds of succeeding.

But that was highly classified information. Other than two terrorist groups, the only people who knew about it were top-ranked Western intelligence officials.

"I'm on medical leave from my university."

Bledshaw nodded. "I know, and you deserve a rest after all you've been through. You've performed a great service for humanity, and you can continue that service as a protector of antiquities. We offer a good pay package, full benefits, a generous retirement fund, and most importantly time to research artifacts that you never knew existed."

That was the hook, and it got her. Over the course of the past few missions, her mind had been blown again and again by the depth and scale of the world's hidden treasures. Radioactive weapons used in ancient Egypt. A perfectly preserved pirate ship. Secret tunnels under the Dome of the Rock. She got the impression that her and Jacob's discoveries had only scratched the surface, that even greater finds awaited them.

And now, here was an organization devoted to finding and studying these things.

If something's too good to be true, it probably is.

That old saying, often repeated by her father when she was growing up, came back to her and made her suspicious.

"So you're U.S. government funded?"

"Yes, with discretionary funds from various intelligence organizations such as the CIA, FBI, and NSA."

That made her even more suspicious. The United States had a proliferation of intelligence agencies, not only the ones he had mentioned but also the BATF, the Department of Homeland Security, and intelligence organizations in each branch of the armed forces. The only thing they all had in common was that they mistrusted each other and often failed to share information. That had led to terrorists getting through before, and from what Jacob had told her, the problem had never been fully solved. Each intelligence agency tried to expand their remit and get more funding, resulting in overlapping jurisdictions and unhealthy competition. Were they really all unified in support of something as obtuse as an Antiquities Division?

And if they were, what the hell was still hidden in the past that Jana didn't know about?

"Um … what would my responsibilities be?"

"Studying existing collections and searching for further artifacts that are endangered. There would be ample time for research. As a Roman specialist, you'll find a great deal in your field of interest."

Jana perked up. "Unknown Roman artifacts?"

Bledshaw inclined his head. "Despite being the best documented ancient society, there is still much about ancient Rome yet to be uncovered."

"What about your existing collection? Can you tell me more about that?"

"I'm afraid that information is restricted to employees. But if you join us in our efforts to protect the world's heritage, then you will be granted unfettered access."

"You're making a tempting offer, Mr. Bledshaw, but a rather vague one."

"I understand you need some time to consider," Bledshaw checked his watch, a gold Rolex, "and I'm afraid I'm in rather a rush. While I would love to discuss this further over lunch, I need to go. Here's my card. Call me any time that you want to meet and talk about the position. I'm looking forward to your call."

Jana took the card uncertainly, and Bledshaw shook her hand and climbed into the back of the Mercedes. The unseen driver drove off, Jana watching them go.

She stood alone in the parking lot for a couple of minutes, having no idea what to think about this odd meeting. Should she tell Jacob? He'd only worry. But sometimes it was good to worry. She felt tempted to call Bledshaw and learn more about this so-called Antiquities Division, but something about the whole thing seem off.

At last, she loaded the groceries in her car and drove off, still wondering.

CHAPTER FOUR

Jacob used a wooden mallet to tap softly on the chisel with a steady rhythm, the wood curling off in thin shavings from what was becoming the arm of a chair.

Jacob's mind was at ease, almost without thought, as he moved with the grain of the wood, bringing out the shape within.

Not the most artistic or complex shape, that was true, but the result was deeply rewarding. He could imagine an object, see it within a block of wood, and bring it out.

Whoever thought he'd have a talent for woodworking? Sure, he was still a beginner, learning off a couple of books and a YouTube series, and yet his first attempts had been pretty good. He'd only been at it for a couple of months. By the end of the year, he'd be making objects worthy of a fine furniture store.

He'd started with simple stuff—bookshelves and a footstool. Now he was working on a pair of armchairs. He still needed to learn upholstery and wickerwork to make the objects he had planned, but those were challenges for another time. Right now he was enjoying the soothing sound and feel that shaping wood gave him.

God, when was the last time he had felt such peace? Childhood? Adolescence? He wasn't sure. It was nice having it back, though.

He heard the front door open. With a smile, he put down his tools, admired his handiwork, and walked into the hallway leading to the front room.

Jana passed through to the kitchen, carrying a couple of bags of groceries.

"You wouldn't believe what happened to me," she said.

"What?" he asked, following her into the kitchen to help unload the groceries.

"Someone tried to recruit me in the supermarket parking lot."

Jacob grinned. "To do what, return the carts? You're overqualified."

"No, for something called the Antiquities Division."

"What's that?"

"Something I've never heard of."

Jana went on to tell of the strange man meeting her in the parking lot, his vague but tempting description of the job, and then she showed him his card.

Throughout her account, Jacob felt a rising sense of concern. This Bledshaw fellow, assuming that was his real name, had obviously been following her. And since he didn't try to kill her, he must really be from some secret government agency.

It pissed him off that they didn't get any warning. Wallace could have called, but Bledshaw had seemed to indicate that Wallace didn't know about the Antiquities Division. What the hell was going on?

"Are you thinking about taking the job?" he asked. The idea unsettled him. It would probably mean a move, and they had created such a bastion of peace here that he didn't want it to end.

"I don't know. He didn't tell me enough for me to make a decision. It sounds interesting, though. I'm wondering about the timing."

"The timing?"

"The dam."

"What dam?"

Jana gaped. "You mean you didn't hear?"

"Hear what?"

"What, don't you look at the news anymore?"

"No. It's all killing and misery. I've had enough of that for one lifetime."

Jana stared at him a moment later, shook her head, and said, "A dam in Nevada burst. Swept away an entire town. They think upwards of ten thousand people died. Initial reports are that it was a bomb."

Jacob's heart plunged to his feet. His stomach clenched. After a moment, he got enough strength to say. "A bomb? It would take a hell of a big bomb to blow up a dam. Was there an airstrike?"

That seemed almost unbelievable, so deep within U.S. airspace, but considering what they'd been through the past few months, anything could be possible.

"The news didn't mention that. Anyway, I'm thinking this Antiquities Division must be involved somehow."

Jacob rubbed his chin. "That does seem like too much of a coincidence. Are you going to call them?"

"I haven't decided yet. Sounds like important work, though. I just wish they hadn't been so hush-hush about it."

"That's how it is in intelligence operations. Need-to-know basis, and they keep you in the dark about everything else."

Jacob felt conflicted. Why were they recruiting her and not him? Sure, she was the archaeologist, but wouldn't they want them as a team? Why split up a winning combination?

He couldn't help but feel a bit jealous. Did they consider her vital and him replaceable? That stung even if he did want to be replaced.

The ringing of a phone snapped him out of his thoughts. It was his encrypted satellite phone, and that meant only one thing.

Tyler Wallace, his boss, was calling.

He rushed to the bedroom to answer.

Punching in the code, he picked up the handset and heard Wallace's voice on the other end of the line.

"Good afternoon, Agent Snow."

Jacob glanced at the clock. Was it afternoon already? He had been losing track of time. It was a good feeling, a luxury he hadn't even known existed before this extended vacation.

"How are you, sir?"

"Recovered from my wound, thanks for asking, and you?"

The Order had attacked his secret residence in Greece. Wallace had gotten injured in the fight while fending off a dozen highly trained operatives. The old guy still had some spark in him,

"Rested, sir. Thank you for this house. Jana and I are both doing well."

"I'm sure you are aware of the situation in Nevada."

"I've been watching it closely, sir."

"We'd like you to get over there and investigate."

Jacob blinked. "Me, sir?"

"Yes, sorry to cut your vacation short."

Actually, I was thinking of it more as a retirement.

"But wouldn't a domestic terror incident be the purview of the FBI or the Department of Homeland Security?"

"They're already on the scene. We'd like someone with your skills as well."

"You're thinking this is The Sword of the Righteous getting revenge?"

"I doubt it. You smacked them down pretty hard and killed their leader. The few remaining elements are on the run or in hiding. Plus the international sweep all leading nations made during the last couple of incidents have put all terror groups on the back foot."

"What about the … other threat?"

Jacob didn't even dare say the name, not when there might still be a mole in the CIA. Aaron Peters, his old mentor and Jana's father, had been hunting down The Order, a shadowy organization behind much of the disruption of the modern world, although they did not seem to have a hand in the nuclear ambitions of The Sword of Righteous. Just exactly what their goals were remained a mystery.

"We're not sure," Wallace said. "It's one of the things we want you to check out. Orders came from on high that you personally should investigate."

Jacob glanced over his shoulder at the closed bedroom door. "What about Jana?"

Wallace chuckled. "You seem to forget that she's not CIA."

"It's hard to remember that sometimes," Jacob admitted.

"The request was only for you. There's a jet waiting for you at the private airport just out of town."

Jacob hesitated. He thought of his woodworking and the batch of beer that was almost done. He thought of the conservatory where they could watch hummingbirds. He thought of long walks in the woods.

And then he thought of ten thousand fellow Americans dying in a terrorist attack.

"I'll grab my bag and get going."

"Thank you Agent Snow. Good luck."

Jacob hung up and cursed. The last thing he wanted to do was go on a mission. He was thoroughly sick of the whole thing. But what could he do? He was still on the payroll. Maybe he should have finished that resignation letter.

Jacob grabbed his bug-out bag and a couple of other things and headed back into the living room.

"Bad news," he told Jana.

"He's sending you to Nevada?"

Jacob nodded.

Jana sighed. "I expected this as soon as I saw the attack on TV. Any idea who's behind it?"

"Nope. That's what I'm supposed to find out."

They embraced and kissed.

"Be careful, OK?"

Jacob flashed her a grin. "Aren't I always?"

"No. Just come back soon, and come back alive."

"I'm not staying in the field any longer than I absolutely have to. I got steaks to cook and a chair to finish."

***

When Jacob's car sped out of sight, Jana sighed and walked back into the house. She felt jealous. Why did he get to go off and check out the dam explosion and she didn't? They were a team. She thought the CIA understood that. She hadn't even been privy to the call.

Perhaps she should talk to Wallace about joining up officially. She'd been on enough missions it wasn't like they could say no.

She sat on the sofa, then sprang up again a moment later. She paced around a bit and turned on the television. The news was only about the disaster. Horrible images of an inundated town and a smashed dam. The talking heads chattered on and on, saying nothing concrete because no one knew anything for sure yet.

Jana switched the TV off and sat down again. Pulling Bledshaw's business card out of her pocket, she studied it for a moment. She set it aside and paced a while longer.

It couldn't hurt to talk to them.

She grabbed the card and her phone and dialed the number.

Bradshaw picked up on the second ring.

"Ms. Peters, how good of you to call."

Great, he's already got my number on his phone. He sure knows a hell of a lot more about me than I do about him.

"Um, hello. I was wondering if we could meet sometime soon and talk over this offer in more detail."

"I'd be delighted. How about now?"

"Um, OK."

"Come to this address. I will treat you to lunch and we will discuss this further."

Jana blinked. In the parking lot, he had told her he was too busy to take her to lunch. Why the sudden change?

He gave her an address. While she wrote it down, she wondered why he didn't simply share the location via Google Maps. Well, he was a bit older. She also wondered why he was still hanging around.

She Googled the address and found it was a private airport just outside town.

"You're at the airport."

"I need to go somewhere, but never mind that. I'll wait to talk with you."

"I'll be there in a few minutes."

Jana grabbed her car keys, hesitated, and then grabbed her Glock 9mm and a spare magazine.

She didn't think he was dangerous, because if he wanted to hurt her he could have easily done so while she was unarmed in the parking lot, but on the other hand she didn't entirely trust him either.

The drive to the airport took only ten minutes. As she passed through the toll gate and parked, she saw a burly man in a nice suit wave to her.

"Good afternoon, Dr. Peters. Mr. Bledshaw is right this way."

Jana kept her distance as she followed him.

They passed through a gate of a chain link fence and came to the tarmac. Not far off, she saw Mr. Bledshaw standing next to a Gulfstream G650 jet, the kind used by executives and tech billionaires. Bledshaw was even richer than he looked, or at least this Antiquities Division was. The CIA had never flown them in such style.

She stopped and stared. Bledshaw was talking to Jacob.

CHAPTER FIVE

"What are you doing here?" Jana asked, stunned to see her lover at the same location the Antiquities Division had sent her to.

"What are you doing here?" Jacob asked at the same moment.

Mr. Bledshaw chuckled. "I hope you'll indulge me in this little ruse. I wanted you both to join up on this mission motivated by your respective passions."

"What's going on?" Jacob demanded.

"The CIA reached out to us because of our specialty to oversee the Harper Dam investigation."

"But you're the Antiquities Division," Jana said. "What's that got to do with a terrorist strike on a dam?"

Bledshaw sighed. "Sadly, quite a bit. If you'll board the plane we can discuss it in the air."

Jana looked to Jacob, who shrugged.

"I got word from the boss to go, so I'm going," Jacob said.

He didn't sound happy about it, and she didn't feel happy about this roundabout way of getting them on the plane either. She didn't think these guys were threats, however, and her curiosity was definitely piqued.

With a last look at Jacob for agreement, she stepped aboard the jet. Jacob followed, as did Bledshaw and the bodyguard. They all sat facing each other over a small table.

They were the only ones in the plane besides the pilot. The jet took off, and once they were in the air, Bledshaw spoke.

"I apologize once again for the way I got you on board, but we at the Antiquities Division only want the best, and only want those who are the most willing."

"You sound like you're recruiting us," Jacob said. "I already have a job."

"Indeed. I doubt the CIA would ever give you up. I'm glad they at least allowed you to join us on this mission. Dr. Peters, on the other hand, is at liberty, and perhaps can be persuaded to join us in common cause to save the world's hidden antiquities."

"Speaking of antiquities," Jana said. "What's the connection between your organization and the Harper Dam?"

Bledshaw opened up a little door in the wall to reveal a liquor cabinet. "Would anyone like a drink? I have some lovely single malt Scotch aged thirty years. Wine too, if you prefer."

"I don't drink on duty," Jacob said.

"It's a four-hour flight, but very well. Jana?"

"A short Scotch for me, thank you." Although she didn't want a drink, Jana decided to act friendly.

Bledshaw poured them both drinks. He didn't offer one to the bodyguard, and the bodyguard didn't ask.

Jana also noted that while the bodyguard had probably spotted her and Jacob's weapons, he hadn't said a word. That reassured her somewhat.

Once they were settled in with their drinks, Bledshaw began.

"As you are aware, a great deal of antiquities went missing during the Second World War."

One of them being the Libyan Staff of Ra, stolen by Rommel. I wonder how much he knows about that?

"Yes, a lot went missing," Jana said and sipped her whiskey. He had as good taste in liquor as he did in tailoring.

"A lot of not only cultural value, but potentially political and military value," he said, looking her in the eye. "After that, the United States government decided to form the Antiquities Division. It was initially made up of the so-called Monuments Men, the famous researchers who recovered artwork stolen by the Nazis and tried to trace the original owners, or at least their surviving families. They had just the right combination of artistic and archaeological knowledge, detective work, and political loyalty."

"I see," Jana said, wondering if political loyalty was the most important thing for Bledshaw on that list.

"For quite some time before the war, there had been those in government circles who realized the importance of some antiquities beyond being simply historic. That only grew after the fall of the Third Reich and the discovery that the Nazis were way ahead of everyone else in this line of research. So the Antiquities Division was set up to collect and study artifacts that had some sort of scientific or defense value."

"You need an entire division to deal with that?" Jacob asked. "Just how many artifacts are we talking about here?"

Bledshaw smiled. "Don't worry, Agent Snow, we're not talking about arsenals of ancient Egyptian atomic weapons or high-tech Roman and Greek devices we're still trying to decipher. There are some of those, certainly—"

"What? Really?"

"Yes, and we aim to keep those safe. There are also a whole host of related artifacts that must be studied in order to understand the most important artifacts. As your archaeologist friend can tell you, context is everything, and it takes a museum's worth of artifacts to thoroughly study any aspect of ancient society."

Jana shifted in her seat. "So what does this have to do with Harper Dam?"

"Sadly, Harper Dam was one of our warehouses."

Jana and Jacob traded a look.

"What do you mean?" Jana asked. "You had some secret room inside the dam where you kept top-secret artifacts?"

She asked this half-jokingly, but the response came deadly serious.

"That's correct. U.S. government interest in secret archaeology coincided with the postwar building boom. A huge number of government projects were launched to add infrastructure to feed America's economic expansion. One of those projects was a series of hydroelectric dams to supply a growing need for electricity. Harper Dam in Nevada was built in the late 1950s by the federal government. Deep inside the structure was a storehouse for artifacts. Only the chief executive of the project knew of it. It does not appear on any public blueprints or records, so even the engineers working there today had no inkling that a secret room existed."

"Wait, if you want to study artifacts, why squirrel them away in the depths of a hydroelectric dam?" Jana asked.

"To keep them safe. While some artifacts are the subject of ongoing study, others have been thoroughly documented but not fully deciphered. They are locked away in the more secure and inaccessible locations to await further study when new insights allow us to learn more."

Jana nodded. This was the logic behind museum collections. A huge amount of archaeological material was stored in museums that rarely got looked at except when someone did a general study of a type of object or a particular period. These things got saved because those general studies could be useful, and future techniques could tease more information out of objects that had already been studied.

“So why put them in a secret room in a dam rather than a warehouse where they’re more accessible for study?”

“Specifically because it is *not* accessible. We have a variety of hiding places, not just dams but other major public projects as well as a few specially made bunkers. Security is paramount, and sadly, most government buildings are less than secure. Remember that intruder who got into the Pentagon?"

The year before, there had been a major scandal when a man used a fake ID to get into the Pentagon as part of a YouTube stunt. That landed the idiot in federal prison. No more YouTube for him.

It also landed the Pentagon security team in some serious hot water.

“So if I join up, I'm going to have to sneak into a bunch of secret warehouses without telling anyone?"

Jacob gave her a double take. He looked surprised that she was considering Bledshaw’s offer. Well, why shouldn’t she?

Although she needed to know more before she could make a decision. A lot more.

“It wouldn’t be as cloak and dagger as all that. We have an excellent computer database of all our objects. You wouldn’t need to study most objects in person although of course that can be arranged.”

“And you have a large Roman collection?”

“We have sizeable collections from all eras and regions.”

“Do other governments have similar projects?”

“Not that we’re aware.”

“So what was in the Harper Dam that a terrorist would want to destroy?” Jacob asked. Jana felt a bit embarrassed to be getting more into the research than the problem at hand.

“A very valuable collection. It’s a terrible loss to world culture.”

While Bledshaw looked legitimately moved, Jana couldn’t help but feel a bit cynical. How could the collection be a loss to world culture if no one except an elite few knew about it? This Antiquities Division seemed a bit like ultrarich private collectors, people who hoarded away Etruscan bronzes and sketches by Da Vinci. They generally did have an appreciation for the cultural treasures they owned, and yet kept anyone else from enjoying it.

“Could you be a bit more specific?” Jacob asked.

“No fissile material. Nothing that would imperil the rescue and cleanup operations.”

“Well, that’s good. What else can you tell us?”

Bledshaw raised a hand. “All in good time, my friends. I understand that I’m being a bit opaque, but neither of you actually work for the Antiquities Division. There is only so much I am authorized to reveal.”

Jana detected a slip. Bledshaw said he was the director of the Antiquities Division, and here he was claiming he needed authorization to tell them more.

From who? The Pentagon? The president?

They fell silent for a time. Then Jacob spoke up.

“So what do you want us to look for?”

"I'm not sure," Bradshaw said. "We're not an espionage organization. Someone of your talents and experience will prove indispensable. We've never been a target of a terror attack before."

“Maybe they targeted the dam and didn’t know about your secret storage chamber,” Jana said.

Bradshaw gave her a sad smile. “I don’t believe in coincidence, and I doubt your companion does either.”

The rest of the long flight was of similarly vague and general conversation that told them nothing other than the fact that Bledshaw wanted their help while keeping them in the dark. At one point, he got a call on a satellite phone, excused himself, and went to the back of the plane to take it.

They fell silent and tried to eavesdrop. Bledshaw spoke in low tones, but they could just make out the words.

And had no idea what they were.

“What language is that?” Jana whispered.

“No clue,” Jacob whispered back. “and I’ve heard most of the world’s languages.”

From most people that would have been a boast. Coming from Jacob, it was a simple statement of fact.

When Bledshaw hung up and came back to his seat, they fell into an uncomfortable silence that lasted the rest of the flight.

CHAPTER SIX

Jacob had seen a lot of destruction in his life. He'd seen car bombs, missile strikes, and the grinding decay of cities torn apart by civil war, but even he was shocked by the devastation of the Harper Dam bursting.

Where once there had been a thick span of concrete fitted with immense turbines reaching from one canyon wall to the other, now there was a gaping hole through which water poured. Only a small stub of concrete remained to either side. Of the great turbines, pipes, and generators, there was no trace.

Bledshaw's private jet flew low over the wreckage, just above a couple of news helicopters. Jacob saw emergency vehicles parked on the road to either side, a road that had once run right over the top of the dam. He wondered why they were there. Anyone working in the dam would have been killed instantly.

"That must have been a hell of a blast," he said, his voice coming out in a horrified whisper. "They would have had to get deep inside and drill holes to set dynamite or plastic explosives. I'm not a demolitions expert, but that would have been a long job and required a whole bunch of explosives. How did they do it without the dam staff noticing?"

"That's one of the questions I hope you'll be able to answer," Bradshaw said, his face grim as he surveyed the scene.

"Have the police arrested any suspects?"

"They've detained a number of people but from what I've heard none are credible suspects. The police are grasping at straws to deflect criticism."

Jacob couldn't blame them. This was the worst terrorist attack on American soil in the nation's history.

The jet banked and followed the course of the river downstream. Jacob's heart sank. He knew what he'd see next.

He felt Jana clutch his hand. Jacob gave it a squeeze but couldn't tear his eyes off the sight below.

A mile downstream, the canyon took a turn, and the cliffs had been battered and eroded by the wall of water that had smashed into it. The clifftop was heaped with debris, mostly chunks of concrete and a mass of twisted steel that could have been part of a turbine although Jacob wasn't sure.

The jet continued, flying as slowly as it could to give the passengers a detailed view of the horror. They spotted several military vehicles along the road, National Guard or maybe troops from a nearby base. Jacob didn't know if there was a base nearby. The government would have called in everybody.

And then they came to the town.

It had stood on a bluff overlooking the river. When the river was dammed, it would have been high and dry. Now the flood had swept it away. All Jacob could see was a tangle of mud, debris, and chunks of concrete the size of houses that had washed all the way down to rest here, after smashing the life out of the town.

After the initial flood, the waters had receded to the original river level from before it had been dammed. Pay Dirt, population formerly 10,000, once again stood above water, but there was no town left. Jacob couldn't even tell where the streets were and where the buildings had once stood. It was now all a uniform mess of death and debris. Only crumbled portions of a couple of concrete high rises remained to show there had been a town there at all.

Jacob could make out emergency workers picking through the mass of mud and debris in a hopeless quest for survivors. They wouldn't find any. No, Jacob was quite sure they wouldn't find any.

He glanced at Bledshaw. The man was pale, his face drawn. Good. He wasn't heartless. Jacob had met a lot of heartless government men in his day. While Bledshaw was still an unknown quantity, he had enough humanity in him to feel the shock of what they were witnessing.

"So now what?" Jacob asked.

"We will land at a private airport in about fifteen minutes. It's generally for small aircraft like Cessnas. Our jet can barely use the runway, but at least the airport won't be clogged by the relief planes being sent by the government. Those are going to the National Guard base. I've arranged a helicopter to meet us at the airport and take us to the site."

"Who's running the relief operation, and do they know you're coming?"

"Right now it's the Nevada National Guard, although every federal agency will be rushing their people in. There will be organizational chaos. There always is in the case of a big emergency, and this is unprecedented. Yes, they know we're coming and we have full authorization to go wherever we need to. We're working under the banner of the CIA for this one."

For this one. It sounded like the Antiquities Division always worked under someone else's name. That would explain why he had never heard of it.

Jana spoke up. "Let's go to where the canyon makes that turn. A lot of debris got washed up on the clifftop. Perhaps we can find a clue."

"Searching for the proverbial needle in a haystack," Bledshaw said.

"Yeah, but it's the only thing we got," Jacob said.

"Very well," the director of the Antiquities Division said.

They landed a few minutes later in a small airport of private planes. As Bledshaw had promised, a helicopter waited for them. To Jacob's surprise, Bledshaw joined went with them. Despite his Ivy League demeanor, it looked like he was taking a hands-on approach with the investigation.

I wonder what this guy's skill set is.

They took off and were soon back at the turn of the canyon that had taken such a battering when the dam broke.

Through their earphones they heard the pilot say, "We're going to have to land a bit away from the cliff, Mr. Bledshaw. It's seriously cracked and eroded."

"Very well, Mark."

The pilot landed half a kilometer away. Jacob, Jana, and the director got out, hunching low and covering their eyes as the blades kicked up a swirl of desert dust. Jacob kept an eye on the ground. He didn't see any cracks here.

But what he did see once they walked away from the helicopter were chunks of concrete and river rocks that had been thrown above the cliff and a full kilometer inland to end up here. What little vegetation there was—a few stubby trees and sparse bushes—had been flattened.

As they proceeded toward the cliff edge, they found more debris and were soon having to clamber over larger stones and fragments of the dam.

Ahead, they saw a hunk of twisted steel with patches of blue paint. It took Jacob a minute to realize it was part of a car.

"Jesus," Jacob whispered. "They had probably been driving along the road on top of the dam when it blew."

“Or the road that once ran along here,” Bledshaw said. “You didn’t see it from the air because it all got eroded away on this stretch. It appears on the map.”

A map that’s going to have to be redrawn.

They didn’t approach the remains of the car. They didn’t want to see what was inside. Nothing living, that was for sure.

“Let’s spread out a bit,” Jana suggested. "We can cover more ground that way. It's like a surface survey in archaeology. Just scan the ground to your left and right and ahead of you, looking for anything unusual."

"I'm not sure anything of interest will have survived," Bradshaw said.

“Neither am I,” Jana admitted. “But it’s a start.”

They kept going, the ground getting rougher and rougher with more and larger pieces of debris. Jacob thanked his luck that they didn’t come across another vehicle. He’d never grown accustomed to seeing civilian casualties.

Then he saw the first of the cracks. It was about as wide as his hand and ran ahead of them a couple of hundred yards to the cliff edge, widening as it went.

Jacob stopped. “I don’t think we should go much further.”

Jana hesitated, looking around. They all saw several more fissures. The ground, which was bedrock just a few inches below the surface soil, had been nearly shattered by the tremendous force of the manmade flood.

“OK,” Jana said, reluctance clear in her voice. “Let’s move parallel to the cliff and see what we can find.”

Jacob shrugged. He didn’t think they’d discover anything of value, but he had no better plan.

They turned left and moved alongside the cliff, keeping about two hundred yards inland. The cracks got too wide, too numerous, and too deep to get any closer.

Bledshaw stopped. “What’s this?”

He bent down and picked up a twisted piece of steel no bigger than his hand.

Jacob and Jana hurried over.

“A portion of guardrail,” Jacob said after a moment.

“My God, it got torn to shreds,” Jana said.

“The pieces must have flown like shrapnel all over the place,” Bledshaw said.

They paused a moment, thinking of the titanic forces that had caused so much destruction.

"Come on," Jana said in a quiet voice. "Let's continue with the survey."

A few steps on, they found a shoe. Jacob averted his eyes, and they continued.

Bits of broken glass that looked like they came from a car windshield, a chunk of pavement with a double yellow line across it, and then a door handle for a car or truck. The three of them walked on in silence, weaving their way between the big stones scattered across the plain.

"At least it was quick for these poor people," Bledshaw said.

"Hey, what's that?" Jana said, pointing in the direction of the cliff.

About halfway to the cliff, something gleamed in the desert sunlight.

"Maybe a bit of glass or a rearview mirror or something," Jacob said.

"No. It looks like metal."

Now that she mentioned it, whatever it was gleamed with a dull golden color.

Jacob pulled out his phone, opened the camera, and zoomed in.

They still couldn't get a good enough look to tell what it was, except that it definitely looked like it was made of gold.

"We should check it out," Jana said.

"I don't know," Jacob replied. "There are some pretty deep cracks over there."

Indeed, the entire surface in that section and all around it was riven with deep fissures.

"It might be important," Bradshaw said.

"I'll be careful," Jana said, moving that way.

"Wait! You can't go alone," Jacob cried.

"Less weight," Jana replied over her shoulder.

"We go together," Jacob said, moving up to her. Bledshaw hesitated and then reluctantly followed.

They approached the golden object. Jacob glanced around and other than a crumpled soda can, saw no other manmade debris.

"Whoa, this really is gold," Jana said. She trotted ahead and stopped at the object. Gingerly, she picked it up. Jacob saw that it was a thin sheet of metal, its edges jagged, with some sort of design hammered onto it. The thing was so battered he couldn't tell much more.

Jana looked at Bledshaw with wonderment.

"This looks like it's from your collection. I'm not sure, but I think it's—"

Whatever she was going to say got cut off by a loud crackling sound. The ground under their feet vibrated, shifted, and sloughed off toward the cliff edge.

CHAPTER SEVEN

Jacob lunged for Jana as the ground slid from under their feet. He grabbed Jana's outstretched hand and got yanked forward as she fell.

He ended up on his knees, feeling the ground shifting like sand beneath him, trying to steady himself with his other hand and not able to get any purchase. Jana was flat on her front, still clutching the gold artifact with her other hand. The ground was shearing off beneath both of them.

Beyond her, Jacob could see the cliff edge drawing closer. It was collapsing, the portion on which they struggled angling down. When that edge got to them, they would plunge several hundred yards into the canyon below.

"Let go of the artifact!" Jacob shouted, struggling to pull her to him, although he wasn't much safer that she was.

Jana didn't listen, trying to worm her way forward, using her elbow instead of her hand as she gripped the gold object.

"Come on, let it go!" Jacob shouted. He knew she loved ancient stuff, but this was getting ridiculous.

He felt a pair of arms grip him around the middle and pull back.

Bledshaw. With surprising strength, he hauled Jacob and Jana back a couple of feet before the shifting ground made him topple backwards. Jacob ended up on top of him.

Jacob grabbed Jana's hand with both of his and flung her a few feet further away from the approaching cliff face. Then he got to his feet, stumbled as the ground abruptly shifted, and grabbed Bledshaw just as he rose. Together they staggered back, hauled up Jana, and stumbled away toward firmer ground.

The collapse of the cliff face sounded like the rumble of a freight train behind them. Their feet slipped on the moving ground, cracks appeared all around them, but they managed to keep going without slipping.

At last they got to a spot where the ground was firm and the cracks weren't widening. They kept running anyway, a full two hundred yards before they collapsed, sweating and panting in the desert heat. The rumble from the cliff subsided, replaced with an eerie silence.

Jacob nudged Jana, who was staring at the twisted bit of gold in her hand.

"That had better have been worth it," he said.

"It's ancient," she said, turning it over in her hand. It was a thin piece of decorated gold about the size of an oak leaf. "I believe it's Parthian."

"Parthian?"

"The Parthian Empire ruled over what's now Iraq and Iran from the third century BC to the mid-third century AD. They were major rivals of the Romans. See this repousse decoration? That's typically Parthian."

There were a series of hammered bumps on the thing that Jacob assumed she meant. Trust Jana to launch into a lecture moments after nearly getting them all killed. He didn't know why that made him love her more, because it should have been seriously annoying, but it did.

"The dam held our Parthian collection," Bledshaw said, wiping his brow. His finely tailored suit was dirty and torn. Jacob spotted the shoulder holster underneath it.

"Why would you have a bunch of artifacts from these Parthian people?" Jacob asked.

"They were a great empire, although the public doesn't know much about them," Jana said. "They also are the source of a mystery thanks to the Parthian battery."

"A battery?" Jacob asked. "I thought this was an ancient civilization."

"It was a surprising find, discovered near Ctesiphon, the old Parthian capital, in 1936. It was a ceramic jar with a bronze tube inside it, and inside that an iron rod. Analysis found that some sort of acidic liquid like vinegar was stored in the bronze tube and the iron rod was suspended in this liquid. Now, if you have two differing metals in an acidic solution, you get an electric charge. That's how modern batteries work."

Another lecture, but this time Jacob was interested.

"So these Parthians created a battery?"

"People doubted that, but more of these batteries have been found. One theory is that they were used for anesthesia. A low-level current acts as a painkiller, and these batteries wouldn't have produced much of a current."

"Huh."

Bledshaw chuckled. “We almost died a minute ago and she’s acting like she’s speaking to a classroom.”

“You’ll get used to it,” Jacob said.

Jana turned to Bradshaw, who sat next to them. All were still panting from their recent ordeal.

“The original battery disappeared during the U.S. invasion of Iraq. Was it in the dam?”

Bledshaw sighed. “Yes, it was, unfortunately. As you know, during the war a great number of artifacts went missing from museums and illegal excavators plundered many archaeological sites. Our organization managed to get much of the material from the black market. We didn’t pay for it, because that would only encourage the thieves, so instead we simply took it.”

“But didn’t return it to the nation that rightfully owns it.”

“For it to get stolen again?” Bledshaw scoffed. “No. You know how the museums in Iraq operate. They leak like a sieve.”

Jana didn’t look happy with that answer, but she didn’t argue with it either.

“So we have some rudimentary batteries and some gold,” Jacob said. “What else did you have in this collection? Anything more high tech? Any security risk?”

“Nothing radioactive. Nothing that would cause a chemical spill downstream. We would have warned the populace.”

Jacob wasn’t sure about that. “Look, I’m not getting much information here. If Jana hadn’t found that bit of gold, you wouldn’t have told us about the Parthian collection at all.”

Bledshaw didn’t meet his eye. “The main thing is to find out who did this.”

“Which we could do a whole lot better if you came clean!”

Bradshaw got saved from having to answer by the helicopter pilot running up to them.

“Thank God you’re all right, sir! I saw the collapse.”

“Yes, yes, we're fine," Bradshaw said, standing and dusting himself off.

“I got a radio message. They would have called you directly, but the cell phone towers were all destroyed in the flood. The dam's security cameras are fed into a security company headquarters in Reno. They're saying they might have found something of interest. They might have spotted the terrorists."

Bledshaw clapped him on the shoulder. “Good work. Let’s go.”

Jacob and Jana got to their feet. Finally, a solid lead.

Bledshaw wasn't going to avoid Jacob's questions forever, though. Jacob promised himself that.

***

Two hours later, in the headquarters of Southwest Security in Reno, Jacob studied the footage with a host of officials from pretty much every federal agency. The president of Southwest Security, a fifty-something Mexican-American named Gonzalez who carried himself like an ex-cop, brought up the footage from a few days before, freezing it where a dam worker was letting a four-man crew in pest control suits carrying spray cans into the subsurface levels of the dam.

"We're thinking the perps are this pest control crew that came in last week. Apparently the dam had a problem with rodents and cockroaches, not surprising considering the wet conditions and workers leaving food out. The regular pest control company had a fire in their offices and lost a bunch of equipment, so the director of the dam called the only other pest control company in the region, a company that we have no record of before last year. We can't even find any proof that they've ever done any business."

The county sheriff cut in. "We're investigating the blaze as suspected arson. We checked on the pest control offices for the other company and found it abandoned, all fingerprints wiped clean."

"Sounds like our guys," Jacob said. "What does the security footage show?"

Gonzalez ran the footage, showing the pest control team spraying the main work areas and setting up traps. Then they went down to the lower levels.

"Here's where things get extra suspicious. The security camera for the lowest level doesn't show any people. We monitor all our clients' properties as well as we can, but since we monitor more than three hundred security cameras for various businesses in the region, we can't keep an eye on everything. Mainly, our people look for suspicious behavior. This footage of an empty room didn't attract notice."

"So is the camera frozen?" the sheriff asked.

"No, It's on a loop. Watch."

Gonzalez pointed to a light bulb in the upper right hand corner. A fly flew into the frame, circled the bulb, and then vanished. Then it flew into the frame again, performing the same maneuver before vanishing again.

"An old trick but a good one," Jacob grumbled.

"The pest control company came four days in a row." Gonzalez ran through several frames from different days. "See how they're carrying large bags? We're thinking that's how they smuggled in drills and explosives. The camera at the security checkpoint shows the security guard didn't search the bags after the first day."

"But the noise, and the time they took," Jacob said. "Surely the dam workers must have noticed. They must have had someone on the inside."

"We've identified one worker, Fred Garrick, who spent the most time with them. Sheriff, you should check his bank account. I bet there was a big deposit in it."

"Did he call in sick on the day of the blast?" the sheriff asked.

"No. I'm thinking the terrorists blew the dam early so he wouldn't talk."

"Serves him right," the sheriff grunted. "I'll put out an APB on Garrick in case he made a run for it. Now let's get a closer look at these perps."

Gonzalez brought up freeze frames showing fairly clear images of all four members of the fake pest control crew.

"One Hispanic and three Anglo," the sheriff said. "All in their late twenties or early thirties, except for that one Anglo guy who looks about fifty. None look foreign to me."

"Sadly, many terror groups include Westerners these days," Bledshaw said.

"Wish you folks at the CIA had found out about these guys beforehand," the sheriff grumbled.

Bledshaw didn't correct him on his assumption that he was really CIA. "It is often the case that terror groups don't announce themselves before making their first big strike. This is because in the past, smaller groups doing smaller attacks attracted unwelcome attention from security agencies and often got taken out before they could make a big hit."

"Oh, yeah, like in the Suez Canal and Jerusalem!" the sheriff scoffed. "You guys have been screwing up big time for a while now. I just lost a whole town in my jurisdiction and you're giving me that load of bull?"

Jacob cut in, keeping a soothing tone. This guy had probably lost friends in the attack. He had every right to be angry, but anger wasn't going to help the situation.

"The CIA has advanced face recognition software. We'll run their faces through the system and see if it gets a hit."

"Who's in the database?" Gonzalez asked.

"That's classified."

"Don't give me that classified crap!" the sheriff barked.

"All known terrorists that we have photos for. Also, everyone on the terror watch list."

Plus every federal and state employee and a whole load of other people, but you don't need to know that.

"Well, get to it," the sheriff said.

"Get me those photos and we'll send them off right away," Jacob said. "Now, if you'll excuse me, I've got to make a call."

Call someone who maybe can help find out who is behind this and who is behind this so-called Antiquities Division.

CHAPTER EIGHT

Aaron Peters was no longer bored. Instead, he was now extremely frustrated. Using his secure computer, he was reading through updates on the CIA server, combing through what little information they had for clues as to who was behind the strike on Harper Dam.

So far, it was a whole lot of speculation and absolutely nothing solid.

He had called in to Tyler Wallace to ask if he could join the investigation and was told that he wasn't needed.

"Get some rest," Wallace said. "You got some serious fights coming up and you need to be in tip top shape."

Wallace was referring to The Order, that secretive organization he'd been fighting for quite some time now. It had infiltrated the CIA and other security organizations, and they were having a hell of a time rooting them out.

So much so that Wallace wouldn't even refer to them by name over a secure, encrypted phone.

So here he was, out of the loop, reading tidbits of information coming piecemeal through the system, and none of it told him anything important.

A call came, not on his satellite phone, but his cell phone.

That was secure and encrypted, too, but not to the same level of security as the satellite phone he used to talk to headquarters.

He looked at the caller ID and saw the contact "Sergeant York." That was the codename for Jacob, named after a movie they both liked. He picked up.

"What's up?" Aaron said without starting with hello. "You working on this?"

Jacob's voice came over the line. "Sure am, but not in the way I thought I would. You ever hear of the Antiquities Division?"

"What's that? Something Jana's doing with her university?"

"Not exactly. Some organization that protects antiquities. Hoards them, more like. The director is a guy named Robert Bledshaw and he tried to recruit Jana this morning. Showed up in the supermarket parking lot to talk to her."

“That’s kind of creepy.”

“It gets weirder. I got an order from Wallace to go to the airport to come down to Nevada as part of the response team. And who do I meet there but Bledshaw with a private jet? Jana had come, too. He had asked her to meet with him but didn't tell her it would be at the airport."

Aaron rubbed his jaw. This sounded suspicious as hell. Interesting, though. He found himself feeling jealous of Jacob’s position. At least he was in the game while Aaron was stuck on the sidelines.

“Huh. So he’s officially working with you and unofficially working with Jana?”

“I don’t know who the hell he’s working with. He says the dam had a secret storage unit for ancient artifacts from something called the Parthian Empire. Never heard of that either.”

“You should have read those books of Roman history I gave you. The Parthians were one of the great military empires of the ancient world. Fought the Romans to a standstill.”

“Whatever. Jana found evidence that that’s true. So Bledshaw is coming clean with some stuff, but he claims he doesn’t know who targeted the collection. He’s convinced the target was the artifacts and not actually the dam.”

“Weirder and weirder. You want me to look into it?”

“Please. I got the registration number of the jet. I’m texting that to you now. We’re in Reno at the dam’s security company, along with a small army of local law enforcement and the feds. It’s a real circus. We got partial face images of four suspects. I sent them in to be scanned. We should have more info soon.”

“Good. I’ll see what I can dig up on the Antiquities Division and this guy Bledshaw.”

“All right. He and his guys have treated us well so far, but he’s not telling all he knows. I’m sure of it. I get the impression that Wallace doesn’t know much either.”

“I’ve never heard of such an organization, but then again I’ve been out of the loop for a while.”

“I’ve been in the loop, and I haven’t heard about it either. That’s what’s got me suspicious.”

"OK. Stay safe, and I'll see what I can find. How's Jana?"

“Eager to get on the trail. We’ve created a monster!”

The two men laughed, although Aaron knew his protégé had as mixed feelings about that as he did.

Jacob hung up, leaving Aaron staring at his phone.

What the hell is going on?

***

Jacob didn't have to wait long for the facial scan results to come back from CIA headquarters. They had made it their number one priority and put as much computing power as they could into it.

Even so, only one face came back with a hit. Jacob read the results on his phone as the rest of the situation room buzzed around them. Jana and Bledshaw were both working nearby. The director of the Antiquities Division had changed into another finely tailored suit to replace the one that got ruined in the landslide.

The hit was for Goran Hribar, a Slovenian mercenary and demolitions expert. He was in his early fifties and in his youth he had worked for whatever side paid the most in Yugoslavia's bitter civil war. Ironic, considering that Slovenia had managed to break away from Yugoslavia with a minimum of fighting and never suffered the carnage that the rest of the former nation did. As a citizen of the new nation of Slovenia, he could have sat out the urban fighting and ethnic cleanings, but instead he dove right in and made a name for himself for efficiency and ruthlessness.

After the war, he had worked for a time with the Russian mob as they muscled into the underworld of the new Eastern Europe, setting off bombs in businesses owned by local mobsters to intimidate them into obeying Russian commands.

Sad. Eastern Europe had thrown off the shackles of Russian political colonialism only to find themselves in the grip of the new Russian mob, and many in that mob had once held high positions in the old Soviet political order.

Goran Hribar had been quiet for the past decade or so, whereabouts unknown. The CIA file said he had possibly retired, but Jacob didn't believe that for an instant. People like that did crime for the thrill as much as they did it for the money. They did not retire.

Jacob also had a hard time believing Hribar would join a terrorist group. His only politics was money, and he wouldn't want to risk his fortune and his life on a high-profile attack for a group whose cause he didn't believe in. Even if they offered him the biggest payout of his career, Hribar wouldn't have thought the potential risk was worth it.

So either Hribar had found a cause—unlikely in Jacob's estimation—or something else was going on.

What that was, Jacob had no idea.

The file said that he had been spotted in a café in Ljubljana, Slovenia's capital, just the day before, talking with some known Croatian arms smugglers.

To have been in Eastern Europe the day before, he would have had to have left almost immediately after his last day doing "pest control" at the dam.

And the other three? He couldn't get a good look at the two white suspects. They could be Slavic, but he couldn't tell. The cameras showed a clearer shot of the Hispanic suspect. He came up clean. No criminal record, no record with INS, no suspicious activity or associates, and no employment on the federal or state level.

That only left Goran Hribar.

He turned to Jana. "You ever been to Ljubljana?"

"No."

"Well, it looks like we're going there now."

Bledshaw nodded. "We can take the jet. We'll have to refuel in New York and again in London, but it will be faster than a commercial flight and we can leave right away."

"All right. We're going to need some equipment."

"I'll provide you with whatever you need."

I'd rather source my own, thank you very much.

"The CIA can handle that. I'll contact the office in Eastern Europe to have gear waiting for us when we land in Slovenia. Do you know that country at all?"

"I was there once ten years ago. I cannot say I know it well."

"Hopefully, the CIA folks over in Europe can find out more about our man while we're in the air. Let's go."

And maybe by the time we get there, Aaron with have figured out who the hell you are and what you want.

Because I got a feeling you're holding out on us and on more stuff than what's obvious.

Oh, yeah. I think you're holding out a whole lot more.

CHAPTER NINE

Jana didn't get much sleep on the plane because Jacob and Bledshaw kept getting on their satellite phones. While in the air, Jacob made arrangements with the local CIA man in Slovenia to bring gear to the airport for them, and the Slovenian authorities were sending along a pair of police officers who specialized in organized crime. All the Western nations were in a panic about the dam strike and feared they might be next. Now, they were all coordinating their efforts and sharing intel. A collaboration that usually would have taken days or even weeks to arrange had been approved in a matter of hours.

Bledshaw spent a lot of time on the phone too, usually sitting in the seat furthest from them, speaking quietly. A couple of times, Jana managed to hear a few words, and they were in that same strange language she and Jacob didn't recognize.

After one of his many calls, he rejoined Jacob and Jana, looking grim.

"We've done some background research on Goran Hribar, the demolitions expert, and we can't find any reason why he'd target our organization. He's in no known terror groups. He's been involved in smuggling in the past, but we believed that he was smuggling arms, not antiquities. And if he wanted our antiquities, why not steal them?"

"You tell me," Jana said.

Bledshaw only shrugged. Jana couldn't tell if his bafflement was real or faked.

His phone rang again, and he went back to his distant seat.

When he returned a few minutes later, he looked even grimmer.

"The terrorists have made a statement. It's a video they posted on a dark web site but it's already leaking to the press. Here, let me show you."

Jacob and Jana crowded around as he put the video on his phone.

The video showed a panning shot of a bare concrete room, the hum of electric equipment in the background. The camera shifted to show some large pipes.

"This is a room in Harper Dam," a computer-generated voice narrated. "We infiltrated this facility in order to send a message to the world." The camera shifted again to show a series of drilled holes in the floor, each filled with a steel tube capped by a detonator. All the detonators were attached by wires to an electronic timer.

The weird, robotic voice continued. "We picked a relatively remote dam for our first strike. The next dam to explode will be a more important one, with a much higher population downstream. You will soon see our power, and you will soon hear our demands."

The video cut off.

Bledshaw turned to them. "I have confirmation that that really was a room in Harper Dam."

"What do they want?" Jana wondered out loud. "They didn't make any demands and they didn't name themselves. All terrorist groups do those things."

Bradshaw shook his head. "I don't understand it either."

"But if they're targeting your collections, why go public at all?" Jacob asked. "And why not embarrass you by exposing you? The Antiquities Division obviously values its anonymity. Since they know of at least some of your secret locations, why not tell them to the world?"

Bradshaw shook his head. "I don't know."

"And how did they find out about you in the first place?" Jana asked.

"We must have a mole. We're currently running an internal review to see who it might be."

Jana and Jacob exchanged a glance. Could it be The Order? That secretive organization had infiltrated the CIA, tried to take Jana hostage, and tried to hunt down her father. Dad said they had infiltrated most Western intelligence organizations and militaries, although the extent of the rot wasn't clear. Maybe they were targeting the Antiquities Division as well.

But why? Despite clashing with The Order several times, they still didn't know what their motivations were.

That made the group all the more dangerous because no one could predict their next move.

"Do you have any secret storage spaces in Slovenia?" Jana asked.

"No."

Jana wondered if that was true. Realizing that getting an answer she'd one hundred percent trust was impossible, she said, "Do you have any idea where they might strike next?"

“I wish I did. We have facilities all over the world. It could be any of them.”

Jana sighed. “Well, I hope we can find this demolitions expert, because otherwise we don’t have any leads.”

***

Two hours later, they sat in a quiet corner of Ljubljana’s airport café with the CIA operative and the two Slovenian police officers. Jacob and the CIA man, an alert older guy who had introduced himself only as Marcus, distinguished themselves by sitting with their backs to the wall. CIA people always did that. Jana wondered if they realized how obvious they acted.

Obvious to her, at least, thanks to her dad’s training. Regular civilians walked around blind.

It was early morning, the café was nearly empty, and Jacob and Jana tucked into breakfast with large doses of coffee.

The two Slovenian officers were a man and woman in their early thirties named Slavoj and Tina. They were in plain clothes, each wearing loose shirts to hide the pistols tucked in their belts. Tina spoke better English than Slavoj, and so she did most of the talking.

"We've been trying to track down the location of Goran Hribar and have come up with nothing. Because Slovenia is in the European Union, he doesn't have to go through border controls and passport checks going to other EU nations. That gets him into Croatia, where he does much of his business. Flight records are checked, of course, but he's too smart to use planes for most trips. We also suspect that he has some false passports since we know he's been spotted in Serbia and Turkey, but there's no customs record of him going there."

“So how are we going to get him?” Jana asked.

“Indirectly. As you already know, he was spotted by our police force right here in Ljubljana just after the attack in your country, sitting at a café with three known Croatian arms smugglers. We've been tracking them, and two have returned to Croatia, but one is still here in town. We think we know where he's staying. I suggest we don't make a big fuss with a police raid, but go in quietly, no uniforms, and try to get him without anyone noticing."

Jacob nodded. “Good plan. We don’t want to alert Hribar to the fact that we’re on his trail. He must suspect we’ll be after him, but there’s no need to make it obvious.”

"Subtlety is the best policy," Marcus said.

Jana smiled at him. "You obviously haven't worked with Jacob, have you?"

"I'm subtle!" Jacob objected.

"Gunshots and grenades aren't subtle," Jana replied.

"No grenades, please," Tina said, apparently unphased. "My government has given you permission for those guns you're trying to conceal, though."

"Thanks," Jacob said.

Marcus said something in Slovenian that Jana assumed was "thank you."

"So who is this Croatian arms dealer and where is he hiding?"

"His name is Nikola Mestrovic. He's been spotted several times having breakfast in various cafes in a certain neighborhood near the castle in the center of town. We believe he's staying at a hotel somewhere there. If he was staying at an apartment, he'd be making his own breakfast. You're in luck arriving when you have. Finish up your breakfast and let's get searching that neighborhood before Mestrovic finishes his."

Jana gulped down the last of her coffee, wished she had time for a third cup, and stood. "Let's get on this."

***

Jana tried to appear nonchalant as she sipped that third coffee she had wanted back at the airport. Slavoj and Tina, the two Slovenian plainclothes officers, had spotted the arms smuggler just up the street, heading this way. The café in which she sat was the only one for a couple of blocks. It made sense that he would come here.

Jana was surprised there weren't more cafes in this neighborhood. She sat at a front window that gave a splendid view of the huge outcropping of rock that dominated the city center, atop which stood an imposing old castle. Jana would have loved the view if she wasn't on the alert for a man whose hands were soaked in blood.

She glanced around the café. A few other early risers sat eating and reading newspapers. Bledshaw sat near the back to cut off the exit through the kitchen. Marcus and Jacob were somewhere outside, staking the place out. The two Slovenians were tailing Mestrovic.

Jana wished she had an earpiece. It would be nice to know how things were going.

She got her answer soon enough. Mestrovic walked through the door.

Jana recognized him from the file photo the police officers had shown them—a big, burly fellow in his athletic thirties and yet with a bit of a gut that spoke of hard Slavic drinking. His eyes darted around the room and immediately spotted Jana, who resisted the urge to look away. That would seem suspicious. Instead she looked him up and down, gave him a smile that bespoke of shy interest, and hid her face with her coffee cup.

Mestrovic's gaze lingered on her body for a moment and then he went to a side table and sat with the least suspicious person in the room—a fragile-looking old lady who was finishing off a plate of sausage and eggs.

One of Mestrovic's contacts? She looked eighty if she was a day. What was she doing in the arms business?

Maybe she's his grandmother.

The waitress came over and Mestrovic ordered breakfast. Once the waitress left, he and the old woman began to whisper to one another.

Jana kept them in her peripheral vision and watched for more newcomers or any suspicious behavior from the other customers or staff. She saw nothing until Marcus and Jacob came through the door.

And then all hell broke loose.

CHAPTER TEN

Jacob entered the café with Marcus just behind. They were sure pretty sure they hadn't been followed. Jacob felt confident that with the two cops as backup and Bledshaw and Jana already in the café, this interception would be quick and straightforward.

He should have known better.

As they came in and Jacob saw Mestrovic sitting with an old woman—the weirdness of that setting off alarm bells in Jacob's head—three things happen at once.

The old woman immediately rose and pulled a Luger and pointed it at them.

A *Luger* of all things. It was almost as much of an antique as she was. Still, her grip was steady, and old guns could kill you just as dead as new ones.

The second thing that happened was Mestrovic rose and charged them. Didn't try to go out the back way, but actually charged them like he was a linesman for the Dallas Cowboys.

The third thing that happened was that a loud bang rang out in another part of the café. Not a flash bang grenade, there was no blinding light, but certainly a big distraction.

At least for those who get distracted by such things.

Not Jacob. He got into a fighting stance, instantly prepared for Mestrovic's attack. Neither man had the chance to draw a weapon.

Jacob tried to land a sidekick against him, but the Croatian blocked, took the impact on his arm instead of his body, and the hefty man's momentum slammed Jacob into the doorframe.

He got a brief glimpse of Marcus going for his gun when a vicious uppercut laid his colleague out flat.

And then it was off to the races.

Mestrovic pelted down the road with as much speed as he had strength. Jacob leaped over Marcus and went after him, his body smarting from the impact to the doorframe. He knew he was going to have a very long bruise from his hip up his side all the way to his shoulder. That pissed him off.

Jacob saw Tina trying to cut the arms smuggler off while Slavoj came down the other end of the street, too far away to get into the game before it went on to its next move.

The next move was Tina pulling out a Taser and firing at Mestrovic.

The guy tucked into a roll that made the pair of electric needles miss, and ended the roll by leaping up and clocking Tina in the jaw.

"That's ungentlemanly!" Jacob shouted.

He didn't hear Jana griping at him for that perfectly valid witticism, so she must have still been inside dealing with that gun-toting granny.

Jacob briefly thought about drawing his gun and shooting this joker in the leg. It would certainly even things up for Tina. The problem was that there were a couple of cars and several pedestrians on the street. If the bullet passed through him, it could ricochet right into an innocent body.

And there had been enough innocent victims already.

Mestrovic didn't draw either, probably because he was too busy running.

Running fast, too. Jacob could barely pace him.

A quick glance over his shoulder told him Slavoj was about ten yards behind, keeping up but not able to close the distance.

So it's up to me. Why is it always up to me?

Mestrovic darted to the other side of the street, cutting across a slow-moving van that honked and screeched its brakes. Jacob cut across behind the van, losing sight of Mestrovic for a second.

The arms smuggler had almost made it to the corner, where a side street branched off out of sight. Jacob figured that was his goal.

Jacob hadn't had time to study the layout of the neighborhood, so he didn't know what was beyond that corner. The only thing he could do was keep up with him and give him less time to disappear or pull some trick.

Then, some good luck.

A young guy came around the corner, staring at his phone and strolling as carefree as you please right into Mestrovic's path.

The Croatian didn't have time to get out of the way. He could only bring his arms up and his head down and body check him.

The young guy flew back, his phone smashing on the ground. Jacob couldn't help but grin.

That's what you get for not paying attention.

The impact allowed Jacob to close the gap a few feet, but he couldn't stop Mestrovic from getting around the corner and out of sight.

Jacob skidded to a stop and pulled out his gun. When you're being chased, getting around a corner and turning right back around to strike at your pursuer was the oldest trick in the book.

He'd used it himself more than once, and the fools who fell for it were regretting their gullibility in the afterlife.

Now armed and ready, Jacob peeked around the corner, pulling back half a second later.

He hadn't seen Mestrovic, only a parked car and a couple of recessed doorways.

The Croatian could be using any one of them as cover.

Leveling his gun, Jacob darted into the intersection, eyes roving.

He ended up behind the nearest parked car and circled around.

Just as he got to the front, getting a good view of the nearest recessed doorway and finding it unoccupied, Mestrovic leaped up from between the two parked cars and hit his wrist with a karate chop. Jacob cried out, and his gun clattered to the pavement.

Suddenly, he found himself facing the muzzle of Mestrovic's .45.

Jacob froze. He should have lashed out, or dodged, but instead he froze.

A man who never froze.

Mestrovic pulled the trigger. All he got was a click.

Misfire.

The Croatian snarled and pistol-whipped him, swinging the heavy steel right across Jacob's face.

Jacob woke up enough to get his arm up, the pain a sharp shock that made him fall against the hood of the car.

Just that moment, Slavoj sprinted around the corner. Seeing the gun, he stopped and pulled out his own.

Mestrovic threw his useless firearm at Slavoj, hitting him in the face and making the police officer stumble back.

The Croatian ran for it as Slavoj tried to recover. Jacob righted himself and looked around for his gun.

Where the hell had it gotten to? He got on his hands and knees and found it under the car. Grabbing it, he leaped up and ran after Mestrovic, only to see him disappear around the corner.

Jacob and Slavoj pursued. By the time they got to the next intersection, Mestrovic was long gone. They ran further, checking the three side streets, and didn't see him anywhere. Cursing, they ran back to the café.

Only to find it in an uproar. Smoke and flames issued out of the front. Tina was helping a burned man out of the shop, a livid bruise on her chin from where Mestrovic had punched her.

Jana was nowhere to be seen.

"Where are Jana and Bledshaw?" he asked her.

"I don't know," the policewoman replied. "I got knocked senseless, and when I came to, the whole place was burning."

"They must have gone out the back way! Let's go," Jacob told Slavoj.

"We'll circle around," Slavoj said.

"No time."

Jacob took a deep breath, held it, and rushed into the burning building.

Smoke hazed the interior. Flames licked one corner of the room, spreading up the far end of the counter. That was the spot where there had been a loud bang. A distraction that had set the whole place on fire.

Jacob ducked as low as possible, still holding his breath, eyes smarting, and rushed through the kitchen. It was abandoned like the rest of the café, but he spotted a bullet hole in the wall and another that had punctured a pot hanging from a rack. He scanned the floor for signs of blood and found none.

The back door hung open. He burst through and took a gulp of clean air. Slavoj followed a moment later.

They found themselves in an alley that paralleled the road in front of the café. Another alley branched off perpendicular to this.

"Damn it!"

He had no idea which way they went.

Slavoj ran to the intersection of the two alleys.

"Look," he said, pointing to a fresh chip out of the brickwork. A scar from a bullet?

They ran down the perpendicular alley, which after twenty yards opened up onto another street. Screams to their left made them turn that way. A small crowd had gathered around a man lying on the ground, clutching his blood-soaked side.

Slavoj flashed a badge and asked a series of rapid-fire questions. A couple of people in the crowd pointed to a distant intersection.

The policeman ran off, and Jacob followed.

When they got to the intersection, they found Jana rounding a corner out of an alleyway.

“Are you all right?” Jacob called.

"Yeah. Have you seen Bledshaw? I lost him during the gunfight. That old woman started blazing away when Mestrovic ran. It's a miracle no one got hit. She retreated through the kitchen and out of the building. We followed, but she put down such a good covering fire that we lost her."

“Well, she can’t have gone far. It’s not like she’s an Olympic sprinter.”

“Maybe not, but she’s deadly with that gun. Who the hell could she be?”

A shot rang out, followed quickly by two more.

“That way!” Slavoj said, pointing. His limited English had left him staring at the two with incomprehension, but the gunshots spoke a universal language.

As they started to run in that direction, another shot rang out.

All they heard after that was silence. The road was abandoned. A few people peeked out from windows or doorways, disappearing immediately as Jacob and his companions passed.

They came to another intersection, glanced around, and saw a bullet hole through the windshield of a parked car. They ran that direction and to their left saw a courtyard.

Bledshaw stood there, gun in hand. The old woman lay dead at his feet. Her gun lay not far off.

They rushed up to him.

“What happened?” Jacob called out.

"I cornered her in this square, and she turned on me. I had to shoot her. She's dead."

Jacob saw a gunshot wound to the old woman's chest and another to the head. The chest wound would have taken her down, so there was no reason for the headshot. The headshot was a killing blow, so there would have been no need to shoot her a second time.

Before Jacob could formulate his suspicions into a question, Bradshaw asked,

“Did you catch Mestrovic?”

Jacob flushed with shame. “No. He got away.”

Got away after nearly killing me. I can’t believe I froze. I never freeze.

What the hell’s the matter with me?

Slavoj got on his police radio. The cops must have already been responding to the running gunfight, and so he was probably calling for a dragnet to try and catch the arms smuggler.

Jacob wasn't optimistic. Someone like that didn't get caught by regular police.

Their only link to their only suspect would disappear into the city. It would take a miracle to track him down a second time.

CHAPTER ELEVEN

Jana sat in an unoccupied corner of the Ljubljana central police station as Jacob, Slavoj, and Tina oversaw the dragnet trying to catch Mestrovic. It had been two hours, and they hadn't found a trace of him. Jana didn't think they would get lucky. The guy had gone to ground. Someone like that probably had plenty of hiding places and allies to spirit him out of the area.

Bledshaw faced her. She had called him over because they needed to talk. Finally. Too many people had died, and they didn't have a clue how to investigate the attack. She needed answers.

"We've lost our one solid lead," she told the director of the so-called Antiquities Division. "If you want me to help, you're going to have to be a lot more forthcoming."

"About?"

"About what was in Harper Dam, what do you think? And what are you storing in the other dams? Do you want my help or not?"

Bledshaw inclined his head. "I apologize for my reticence. It's just that we've been so protective of our collection, so secretive for so many decades."

"That secrecy isn't working anymore. You obviously have a mole in your organization. You hired me to help, and I do want to help. But I can't do that unless you come clean with me."

Bledshaw paused, considering what she said. Jana tried not to show her frustration. This is something that had always irritated her about secret government organizations. Her childhood and youth had been constantly disrupted by her father's long and frequent absences, when he could never tell her how long he'd be gone or even where he was going.

The exotic presents he brought back for her didn't compensate. She always suspected he got them at airport shops on his way back, not in the places he actually went.

This got confirmed when he came in from the cold and she learned that he had spent most of his time in Pakistan and Afghanistan. None of her gifts had come from there. Instead, they came from England or Japan or the Philippines.

Tactical obfuscation. That was the term. And he had used it on his own daughter.

She had come to forgive him all that. Aaron Peters had been saving the world, after all. Jana was far less certain of Robert Bledshaw's motives.

Jana and Bledshaw had been staring at each other for a few seconds now. Bledshaw blinked first.

"Oh, very well. Harper Dam was our storehouse for Parthian artifacts, as I mentioned. You see, I haven't been entirely obfuscatory, although I see now that I should have been more forthcoming."

"No time like the present," Jana grumbled.

"You're right. The Parthian collection had many examples of ancient technology, much like the Staff of Ra."

Jana tensed at the mention of that top secret artifact. Only the CIA, other Western intelligence agencies, and a couple of terrorist groups knew of its existence. Bledshaw had just proved that the Antiquities Division was as well-connected and well-informed as he had boasted.

Bledshaw went on.

"The Parthian batteries were only the tip of the iceberg, if I can use such a metaphor in reference to the Middle East. There was an excavation in Iran in the 1990s that uncovered an entire Parthian research laboratory where they had experimented with running electrical current through copper wires, constructed batteries far more powerful than those produced by previously known examples, and had made great advances in optics and astronomy."

"And why have I never heard of this excavation?" She asked that not because she doubted its existence—nothing surprised her anymore—but because she wanted to know how they had kept it a secret.

"The Iranian government wanted to publicize the dig, but they were convinced not to."

"By who? You?"

"Not me personally. I was only a junior employee at the time."

"But the Antiquities Division?"

"Yes."

"And how did you convince the Iranian government not to talk about it? How did you get the artifacts?"

"We made a trade. We gave them modern technology for ancient technology."

“Wait. What? Isn’t there an embargo on Iran? You can’t give them technology.”

“Surely your work with the CIA has taught you that rules are meant to be broken.”

“It’s one of the worst regimes in the world! Next you’ll be telling me you sent missiles to North Korea.”

“We haven’t made any deals with North Korea, and we didn’t give the Iranians anything useful.”

“What do you mean?”

Bledshaw smiled. “They wanted gyroscopes for their missile systems, very precise ones from an American company forbidden to do business with them. We had the company make up some very convincing fakes. They worked, but were made of inferior materials so they broke under the stress of flight. By the time they tested them in flight instead of just in the lab, all the artifacts were safely out of the country.”

Jana chuckled at that, then grew serious. "So, do you think the Iranians did this?"

“Doubtful. No state would launch such a severe attack on American soil. It would mean its annihilation.”

“But wait. Harper Dam is decades older than that deal. What did you store there before?”

“Sri Lankan artifacts. They were moved some time ago.”

“What artifacts? And why did you move them?”

“That’s irrelevant.”

“Maybe the attackers thought they were still there.”

“They didn’t.”

“How do you know?”

“I know.”

Jana sighed. “I thought you were going to be cooperative.”

“I’m trying to be. There are limits to what I can reveal.”

“Go on.” She was losing patience with this guy. In fact, she was losing patience with this whole situation. But what could she do? Walk away?

“The Parthian collection was an extensive one, not just the items from the ancient laboratory but also a number of texts and artifacts from various other sites. I’ve been given permission to let you access that portion of the database. Perhaps you can discover what it was they wanted to destroy. It strikes us as odd that they would want to wreck the collection rather than steal it. As antiquities, they are priceless. As weaponry or covert intelligence, they are of no value. There is no reason why some entity would want us not to have them if they weren't going to take the artifacts for themselves."

"But if they wanted to destroy them, they could have used less explosives than they did," Jana pointed out. "They could have disintegrated everything in that storage room without bursting the dam and killing 10,000 people."

"You're quite correct. I'm not sure why they chose this path. It seems … "

Tina approaching them made Bledshaw stiffen and stop talking. The Slovenian policewoman had noticed they were having what looked like a private conversation and had hesitated some distance away. The buzz of the busy station sounded behind her. Bledshaw motioned for her to approach.

"We've discovered the identity of the dead perpetrator. Ana Hroj-Mihic has dual Slovenian and Serbian nationality and is the widow of a Serbian mob boss. I'm assuming Mestrovic was meeting with her to arrange some sort of arms deal. Her husband made a fortune in that business after the fall of Communism. We haven't yet located Mestrovic, but we've arrested several known associates of Hroj-Mihic and hope to make them talk."

"Any sign of Goran Hribar?" Jana asked. "He's the person we were originally looking for, after all."

Tina shook her head. "We've informed all the airports, bus stations, and borders, but I doubt that will work with someone like that."

"Damn it," Jana muttered. "Well, I better get cracking on that collection information. Robert, send me the data."

Tina looked at her curiously and then walked away.

After she left, Bledshaw held up a memory stick. "It's on here."

***

An hour later, Jana was still entranced. The collection hidden in the deep recesses of Harper Dam changed the scientific view of one of the world's most important ancient civilizations.

And yet, no one had heard of the findings.

It was all there, everything Bledshaw had mentioned and more—the batteries, the copper wires, the long inscriptions detailing an extensive knowledge of astronomy and mathematics. There were treasures too—gold masks and armor, jewelry and fine sculpture.

Priceless. A treasure trove of historical information and art. Why would someone want to destroy it? There seemed to be no reason. What a waste.

What annoyed her almost as much as the collection's destruction was how it had been hidden from the world in the first place. This collection belonged in a museum, preferably in Iran. It was their heritage, after all. But the Iranian government had callously given it up in exchange for what it thought was a part for a missile system. Typical. Pre-Islamic antiquities held little value for that regime.

So she agreed with Bledshaw's assessment that the Iranians didn't hit the dam. The deal had been almost thirty years ago. If the Iranian government had dared to strike, they would have done so then, not now. And such a bold step would have meant war, a war the Iranians would have lost with catastrophic consequences.

So that got her back to square one. Who blew up the dam and why?

The answer must be in this collection somewhere …

She continued to scan through the list of artifacts on the read-only file. Jana had noticed that it was set so she couldn't copy the file, she couldn't even highlight text to copy and paste it. The Antiquities Division might be allowing her a glimpse of their collection, but they weren't going to share that information with anyone else.

And if she told her colleagues what the Antiquities Division had hidden inside Harper Dam, none of those archaeologists would have believed her.

There was a knock on the door. Bledshaw had insisted that she lock herself in a spare office while she read through the database.

"Who is it?"

"Me," Jacob called.

She got up and unlocked the door. "Come on in."

He entered, closing the door behind him.

"How's it going?"

Jana shrugged and gestured helplessly at the screen. "It's an amazing collection, but it's not giving up any clues. Anything new from the police?"

"I wish there was." Jacob sat down next to her and gave her a kiss. "Does that help?"

"Well, it makes me feel better," she said with a smile. "But it doesn't get us any closer to the answers we need."

"Maybe there's a link between this collection and one of the others they're hiding away."

"That's what I'm thinking, but since Bradshaw won't tell us anything about the other collections, it's impossible to figure out."

"He's not exactly the most cooperative man I've worked with."

"You can say that again," Jana grunted.

"He's not exactly the most cooperative man I've worked with."

Jana elbowed him. "Be serious. The only thing I can think of is that there's a link with advanced technology. He knew about the Staff of Ra, and the collection in Harper Dam shows the Parthians were way more advanced than we thought."

"Why would someone destroy evidence of advanced technology instead of steal it?"

"Damn good question. I was asking myself the same thing."

"Well, let's look through this together. There's nothing much for me to do with the police investigation. It's all in a language I don't understand."

"Like that weird language Bledshaw uses on the phone."

Jacob lowered his voice. "Another mystery he won't reveal. I don't trust the guy. My gut tells me he shot that old woman because he didn't want her to talk. I have no proof of that, but I got a pretty strong suspicion."

"It sure is a possibility," Jana said, feeling a chill run through her.

Together, they went through the collection catalog from the beginning, examining each piece in detail and looking for any possible connection to something larger. They stayed silent, sitting side by side, reading through the entries.

"Let's focus on the inscriptions," Jacob suggested. "Maybe they mention contacts with other civilizations."

"Good idea. I haven't done anything but skim the inscriptions yet. There are so many."

They started looking through the inscriptions.

The first couple of texts referred to motions of the planets and predicting eclipses. After that, they studied another text that discussed the principles of electricity in a vague but nonetheless accurate manner. Jana was amazed the Parthians had developed so far along those lines.

Then they hit the jackpot.

"Here," Jana pointed. "They're talking about hiring craftsmen from Pataliputra to work in their laboratory, perhaps the same laboratory that was excavated in the Nineties."

"Where the hell's Pataliputra?"

Jana was just about to answer when Bledshaw burst into the room, his face pale and drawn with worry.

"The terrorists have made another threat and stated their demands."

CHAPTER TWELVE

Jacob shoved through the assembled crowd of Slovenian police to stare at the computer screen where a video was playing. It was a montage of news images of the destruction of the Harper Dam and the flooded town of Pay Dirt. Over these terrible images spoke a computer-generated voice.

"The first attack was a warning. The second attack will show we are in earnest. Far, far more people will die. Our second target will be a dam upriver from a major urban center. When the dam blows, the water will rush down and drown hundreds of thousands.

"Or not. The choice is yours. All we want is the Curator. Hand him over at the coordinates now scrolling on the bottom of your screen and we will stop the attacks. You have twenty-four hours. If you do not hand over the Curator, we will blow the dam and blow another dam every twenty-four hours until you obey.

"Millions of innocent lives are in your hands. You can save them all by simply giving up one single individual.

"The clock is ticking."

Jacob leaned over, studying the coordinates scrolling across the screen. A policewoman was already typing them into Google Earth.

"Siberia!" she cried.

Indeed, the coordinates were in north-central Russia. The policewoman zoomed in and found the spot was literally in the middle of nowhere. The nearest road was miles away, the nearest settlement even further. There was nothing but taiga and a couple of rivers.

"I bet the Russians are involved," Tina said.

"This might be misdirection," Jacob replied.

"Who the hell is this curator they're talking about?" one of the other Slovenians who spoke English said.

Jacob and Jana both looked at Bledshaw, who shrugged. "I have no idea."

"Nonsense," Jacob said. "Your organization has its own private archaeology collection. You must have a curator."

Tina's brow furrowed. "The CIA has an archaeology collection?"

“Yes,” Bledshaw lied, then frowned at Jacob, who realized that he had let slip one of Bledshaw’s private little secrets. Jacob felt like shouting it to the whole world.

Jacob hooked his arm around one of Bledshaw’s and moved him away from the crowd. Jana followed.

Jacob led them back to the office and closed the door behind them. Then he rounded on Bledshaw.

“OK, enough bullshit. Who’s this curator they want?”

Bradshaw raised his hands. "We don't have anyone bearing the title of curator."

“Tell us the truth! These people will blow another dam.”

“You think I don’t know that? You think I don’t want to stop them? I’m the one who reached out to you, remember? But there’s no one in the Antiquities Division with the title of curator. We have myself as director, a couple of assistant directors, and a warden for each collection. We also have researchers and epigraphers to study the collection. No curator. That's a museum term, and we aren't a museum."

“I’ll say,” Jana growled. “You want to keep everything for yourself.”

“It’s necessary,” Bledshaw said in a softer tone.

“Why?” Jacob demanded.

“Because the secrets we hold cannot be allowed to be known by the general public, or even academia.”

“Like what?” Jana asked. “There’s nothing in the Parthian collection that would have caused international instability, but blowing up Harper Dam certainly has.”

Bradshaw shook his head. "I wish I could tell you, but I'm not allowed. You're a professor."

Jacob got in his face. "Enough of this. I want some answers, and I want them now. Who is this curator and why does this organization want him or her so bad?"

“There is no curator. And as for the terrorists’ motives, I don’t understand them any more than you do. It makes far more sense to steal the collections.”

“Do you have any idea which dam they might hit next?” Jacob asked.

“No.”

“I do,” Jana said.

They turned to her.

“Just before you came in, I saw one of the inscriptions referred to Pataliputra. That was the capital of the Maurya Empire, which ruled over much of India during the same period the Parthians ruled over what’s now Iran and Iraq. It was an advanced empire with a focus on science. Apparently the Parthians used Mauryan expertise. If it’s ancient technology the terrorists are targeting, that would be a likely candidate. Do you have a Mauryan collection?”

To Jacob’s surprise, Bledshaw actually answered honestly.

“We do. It’s in a dam in northern India.”

“Does the Indian government know about it?”

“No.”

“Jesus! Well, alert the dam with whatever bullshit story you already got in your head and let’s get going,” Jacob said.

“I will. We’ll take the jet there. On the way, you can search through the Mauryan database and see if you can find something significant. Personally, I can't see what they'd be after that. Also check the rest of the Parthian database for more clues."

Suddenly, Jana looked unsure of herself. "It's a pretty tenuous connection, just a mention in one of the texts saying they were hiring some Mauryan specialists to work in the laboratory. I seem to remember that a couple of other texts mentioned the Mauryan Empire as well. But it might not be anything.”

"I think it is," Bradshaw said. "For some reason these terrorists want to destroy evidence of ancient electricity, or perhaps ancient advances in technology in general."

Jacob and Jana exchanged a look. They had no idea why someone would want to do that, but since Bradshaw obviously knew more than he was letting on, his assessment might very well be correct.

***

Agent Twelve looked at Agent Zero with even greater admiration than he ever had before. He had masterminded the blowing of Harper Dam, whisked him back to Eastern Europe, and then smuggled him to a remote headquarters and safehouse on Turkey’s Black Sea coast.

Agent Twelve’s real name was Goran Hribar, but no one in the ops room knew that except Agent Zero.

Agent Zero knew everything.

He watched him now, an older American gentleman with thinning hair who wore an expensive tailored suit and emanated a sense of confidence and command. He stood behind a bank of computers while three other agents brought up dam schematics from around the world, encrypted Dark Web communications, and the latest news from half a dozen nations.

"Agent Seventeen, any update on the operations in Bihar?" he asked.

"Bledshaw and his CIA contacts are on their way to Patna Dam and the ambush is ready."

Agent Zero nodded. "Good. Very good."

"With any luck, we'll wipe them out," Goran Hribar/Agent Twelve said.

"Unlikely. Jacob Snow and Jana Peters are highly capable and have survived far worse than what we are going to throw at them in India. The ambush will only convince them they're on the right track. That is good enough. Deception is the best weapon against people like that, not brute force."

"I can blow them into a thousand pieces any time you want."

"In time, Agent Twelve, in time." Agent Zero turned to another computer bank.

"And as for the demolitions guy you got for the Patna Dam … "

"He is perfectly sufficient for our needs," Agent Zero said in a soothing voice.

Agent Twelve shrugged, accepting his superior's assessment. This guy knew the overall operation far better than he did. One thing he liked about Agent Zero besides his obvious capability was that you could bring up reasonable objections. He wouldn't scream and stomp and tell you to shut up like some of the Serbian and Croatian generals he'd known back in the civil war, and while he wouldn't always go along with your point of view, he would always listen. That was a sign of confidence, a key ingredient in good leadership.

Agent Zero turned to a young Turkish woman tapping away at a keyboard. "And how does our second operation proceed, Agent Twenty?"

The young woman at that computer said, "Social disruption is rising dramatically. The various departments of the central government are spending so much time blaming each other and fighting over who's in charge of the defense and evacuation duties that they're tripping themselves up. It's all chaos over there."

"Perfect. Chaos is what we want, in the short term at least."

Agent Twelve smiled. He knew all about chaos. The Yugoslav civil war had been the bloodiest conflict Europe had seen since World War Two, a nasty three-way civil war that had plunged the Balkans into chaos.

But from that chaos had come opportunity. It had led to the creation of new nations and new fortunes, including his own fortune.

What he was involved with now was on a whole other level. There would be far more chaos, and far more opportunity.

And fortune? Agent Twelve, aka Goran Hribar, smiled. Oh, there would be fortune for him in the new order that would arise out of that chaos, but there would also be something far greater, far more desirable that he had never enjoyed before.

Power.

Agent Zero would give him power.

CHAPTER THIRTEEN

"Here's the schematic of the Patna Dam," Bledshaw said, setting a tablet down in front of Jana and Jacob. "Sorry, it took so long for me to gain approval to show it to outsiders. We have our own level of bureaucracy, and being the director does not save me from it. I'm sure you are familiar with that, having worked with the federal government."

Jana rolled her eyes. The delay on something this crucial had been interminable. They had already boarded Bledshaw's jet, passed over the Mediterranean, the Sinai, down the Red Sea and stopped to refuel at Dubai. Now, they were crossing the Indian Ocean heading for the Indian city of Patna.

While the ancient Mauryan capital of Pataliputra had been abandoned for centuries, the good geographic location meant that the more modern city of Patna had grown up on the same site. It was now the capital of Bihar state in northeastern India.

Jacob edged closer so he could get a good look at the schematic. It felt nice having him so close. While Jana had been glad to see him so relaxed back in Virginia, he had been a bit unfocused, listless even. The old Jacob Snow was back.

“Will the dam bursting flood Patna?” he asked.

“Unfortunately yes,” Bledshaw said.

“How many people live there?” Jana asked.

"The entire metro area has a population of almost four million," Bradshaw said. "Plus the towns and villages between the dam and the city.”

Jana shuddered. “My God.”

She had dealt with large-scale threats before, including a nuclear device that almost went off in central Rome. This, however, seemed worse. It wasn’t some group with a hidden bomb, but a country’s own infrastructure being turned against them.

Together, they looked at the schematic. Jacob moved the view around and zoomed in on the access points.

“How good is security?” he asked.

"Decent in regular times, cast iron now. An entire regiment of the Indian army has arrived to guard the place, complete with air support and high-speed boats on the river and reservoir."

"Did they find a bomb?" Jana asked.

"No."

Jana looked at him. "Did they find your secret room?"

Bledshaw gave a tight smile. "There's little chance of them doing that."

Jana gestured at the tablet. "Yeah, it doesn't even appear on your own schematic."

"Ah. An oversight. Forgive me." He took the tablet, punched in a code he hid from them, and placed the tablet back on the desk.

The schematic now showed a room below the lowest one. Jana didn't think for one second that Bledshaw had forgotten to show it to them. He had done the very male and very annoying thing of showing off his knowledge and power.

That didn't impress her, not after all she'd been through. Instead, it only made her trust him less.

They studied the schematic. From the engineering room on the lowest level, there was a narrow staircase leading down twenty feet to a large room, about the size of a convenience store.

"How do you get inside?" Jana asked.

"The entrance is hidden in the floor. To access it, you have to punch in a long key code into the engineering control panel. There isn't a chance that someone could do it by accident, and the way the wiring is laid out, even if one of the engineers noticed it, they would assume it led to one of the power sources. It's all but impossible to find."

"And the terrorists don't even need to find it. All they want to do is blow it up," Jacob said.

Bradshaw shook his head and grimaced. "And we thought hiding the collection in dams would keep them safe. While we use many hiding places, our most important collections go in secret chambers in hydroelectric dams. Built to last, closely guarded, and hard to destroy, we thought they would be the perfect hiding place."

Jacob's scratched his jaw. "If this is their next target, why haven't the Indians found the bomb? I'm sure they've scoured the place."

"I don't know," Bledshaw admitted. "Perhaps they hid it."

"We only had a tenuous connection between the Parthian collection and the Mauryan collection," Jana said, unsure of herself.

"It's the only connection we have," Jacob replied. "And security has stepped up at dams around the world. Wallace called me while we were at the police station and told me dozens of nations have ordered searches of all their dams."

"Well, if they haven't found anything yet, then either this group is attacking a dam they haven't checked or they're hiding their charges somehow," Jana said.

That got them studying the schematic.

The dam near Patna had a conventional layout. The dam itself, a mass of concrete that was sheer facing the lake and sloped on the other side to act as a buttress, had a flat top and a small building on top with monitoring devices and another engineering level below that. Unlike with the Harper Dam, no road ran atop it. Deep below the dam was the intake, a large screened entrance for the water to flow through a channel called the penstock. The penstock channeled the water, making it hit the turbine and spinning it to generate electricity. After that, it flowed out into the river.

Jana saw three possibilities. The best place for access was the powerhouse, where the generator sat atop the turbine. There was a mass of electronic equipment and power cables that ran from the powerhouse out to the city of Patna and the surrounding area. That offered the easiest access but was also guarded and easily checked. She had no idea if it was possible to hide a bomb large enough to blow up the dam in that building. Also, since it was somewhat separate from the dam's main structure, would a bomb there even destroy the dam?

The second possibility would be to have an underwater demolitions team on the reservoir side plant explosive into the concrete there. That seemed like a tough operation to keep secret and presumably the Indians had sent their own divers down to check on that.

The third possibility is that they access the secret collection room below the engineering level. It was, after all, the deepest level in the dam structure itself, a perfect place to plant a bomb. It offered a place out of sight of the dam's staff where a demolitions team could drill holes into the concrete and fill them with explosives.

They hadn't done that with Harper Dam, but they might have at the Patna Dam, which was much larger. It would take more explosives, sunk deeper, in order to burst it.

She relayed her observations to the two men, and they nodded.

"That's exactly what I was thinking," Jacob said. "Damn, you're good at this."

Jana smiled at the compliment, but the smile didn't last long. Far too many lives were at stake.

"So do you think they snuck into your collections room?" Jana asked their mysterious host.

"Impossible."

"A week ago you would have thought it impossible for them to know about these collections at all, but they obviously do."

"Even if they knew the room was down there, how would they know it was accessed by a key code, and how would they know the combination?"

"Maybe that mole you think is responsible knows the combination," Jacob suggested.

He's talking about The Order.

That organization had infiltrated the CIA and several other governmental bodies, so why not the Antiquities Division?

Bledshaw made a dismissive wave. "Impossible. We've vetted everyone very carefully, and in any case, no one has that knowledge. Also, we have no missing personnel."

"Well, if the Indians haven't found a bomb, then it can't be underwater or in the powerhouse, so it has to be in your secret chamber."

Bledshaw's features tightened and he didn't respond for a moment.

"What about an airstrike?" he said at last.

"I suppose that's possible," Jacob replied. "It would take at least a couple of well-armed warplanes, either bombers or fighters armed with heavy missiles. Not sure where your enemies would get those, and from that report you shared, the Indian government is patrolling the skies. The Indian Air Force is pretty good. Not at U.S. or Russian levels, but good enough to stave off a threat like that."

Jacob glanced at a digital readout on the wall that gave the times in various world capitals. "So we know a whole lot less than what we do know. Story of my life. At least we have some time once we get to the dam to locate and defuse the bomb. You sure you don't know who this curator person is?"

"I haven't the faintest idea. I wish I did. Just because we were targeted by the blast doesn't mean we are the target of the demand."

That's not how terrorism works, buddy.

Jana decided not to say anything. They'd only get more obfuscations.

And those obfuscations were getting really, really annoying.

Could she actually work for someone like this? She supposed he'd be more forthcoming if she was actually an Antiquities Division employee, but that might only lead to a new level of secrecy, like with the CIA. Jacob was constantly discovering things he didn't know about his own organization.

She didn't want that kind of lifestyle.

But to have access to a secret treasure trove of the world's finest artifacts …

Jana wasn't sure she could resist the temptation of joining, even though her instincts told her there was something very fishy about this whole operation.

The pilot came on over the intercom. "Ladies and gentlemen, we have a strong tailwind that's helping our speed. Indian air control is giving our plane priority for landing, so we should land at Patna airport in a little less than an hour. The Indian military will have a helicopter waiting to take you straight to the dam. They'll get you to the dam well before the deadline."

Bledshaw nodded with approval and muttered, "Good."

Jana didn't feel so optimistic. While they may have some extra time, they still had to find the bomb, something the Patna Dam staff and the Indian army had failed to do, and then figure out a way to defuse it.

Jana settled back in her seat and tried to relax. She needed her rest. She had the feeling that this would be her last chance for a long, long while.

CHAPTER FOURTEEN

Jacob studied the dam as the Indian Army helicopter touched down right on top of it. There was no helipad, and the top was a bit too narrow for the heavy military chopper, but someone on the ground had painted markings and the pilot touched her down with perfect precision.

He hoped the rest of the mission would go as smoothly.

They had been met at the airport by Major Parminder Singh, a beefy Sikh who stood six-foot-four and carried an assault rifle slung over his shoulder despite being an officer and flanked by similarly armed privates. After a brief round of introductions, he had whisked them onto the helicopter and brought them straight here.

"We are most happy to have your expertise," the major said in the lilting tones of Indian English. "We have searched the dam thoroughly, and sent frogmen into the reservoir. We have also closed the penstock and checked inside. We can find no trace of a bomb. Are you sure this is their next target?"

"We're not sure of anything, but one lead points to this particular dam."

A pretty thin lead, Jacob admitted to himself. *But Jana's gut tells her it might be here, and trusting her gut has solved a whole lot of problems in the past.*

"Our forces have conducted equally thorough searches on all other dams in the country with no result. Why would they target the United States and then India? Are they Islamic terrorists? Their demand for this Curator person seems atypical of Islamists."

"We're not actually sure who's behind the attacks," Jacob said, glancing at Bledshaw, who said nothing. *Although one of us might have a better idea than I do.*

They filed out of the helicopter door, hunching low as the rotor blades swirled the air around them. Bledshaw's bodyguard accompanied them.

Jacob glanced around and saw he was superfluous. Guards and armored cars were posted at either end of the long concrete span, while snipers and men with Stinger antiaircraft missiles stood at regular intervals in between. A circle of half a dozen army helicopters hovered around the dam, and further up in the sky he could see three fighter jets. The Indians were taking the threat seriously.

Major Singh led them to a small concrete building near one end of the dam. His two privates came along. Once they were inside and crowded into an ops room with a series of monitors, it was quiet enough to speak. A couple more guards stood there, as well as a middle-aged man in a hard hat.

"We are at your service. As you can see, we have the dam thoroughly guarded. All employees have been searched and are escorted everywhere by an armed guard. Here is the dam manager, Bahadur Rao."

The man in the hardhat shook everyone's hands. "I can take you anywhere you wish to go. Where in the dam do you think the terrorists will strike?"

"We're not sure," Jacob said, "but the Harper Dam was blown at its lowest level with charges of high explosives drilled into the wall and floor."

Bahadur Rao shook his head. "There has been no such drilling here. My staff has made a thorough search, and so have the police and military."

You searched all the places you know of.

"How about we check the lower levels of the dam," Bledshaw suggested.

The manager shrugged his shoulders. "There isn't much in the dam structure itself. Most of the rooms are in the power station."

"Yes, but to blow the dam, the explosives would have to be set here."

"True enough."

Rao led them to a staircase. Major Singh, his two privates, and Jacob's team followed.

Or was it Robert Bledshaw's team? Jacob wasn't quite sure.

They clanged down a narrow steel staircase into the bowels of the dam.

"Here we have various onsite monitoring systems and the concrete is thoroughly checked for microfissures or flaking," Rao said as if giving a tour. "We are proud that we have received top ranking in the India Hydropower Industry Awards three years running."

"Have you had any new employees join in the past year?" Jacob asked.

"One, an engineer. He has been thoroughly checked, as have all my other employees. There is no sign of suspicious activity."

"What about outside contractors?" Jana asked. "The Harper Dam was blown by a terrorist team posing as exterminators, brought in by an accomplice on the inside."

"We have not had any outside contractors come in for more than three months. We did have a government inspector come in for his monthly inspection, but he was accompanied by myself and my chief engineer the entire time and he only stayed a couple of hours. There was no way he could have planted the charges."

They came to a long, low room full of humming machinery Jacob didn't recognize. A pair of bored-looking Indian soldiers stood guard, snapping to attention the instant they saw a superior officer. Jacob smiled. The American army experience wasn't much different. You got ordered to do a dull job and had to pretend to be eager whenever the brass came around.

Remembering the schematic, Jacob said,

"Let's go to the next level down."

"You mean the lowest level."

What you think is the lowest level.

They went down another flight of stairs and ended up in a smaller room with a large bank of complex electronics. A half dozen soldiers stood guard here. Jacob wondered why there was so many. From the puzzled expression on Major Singh's face, he thought the same.

He asked a question in Hindi, and the men replied.

"There's the keypad over there," Bledshaw pointed.

"Why do you wish to examine the keypad?" Rao asked.

The dam manager never got the answer to his question, because all six of the guards in the room leveled their guns and opened up.

Jacob threw himself on the ground, rolled, and drew his pistol. He had a fleeting glimpse of Rao and Major Singh's two privates stagger and fall, torn apart by bullets, and then he was firing back.

His first shot took one of the terrorists right between the eyes. His next bullet was a gut shot that doubled the man over. Bullets whined in the air all around them, and Bledshaw's bodyguard took a headshot. Major Singh unslung his assault rifle, took a bullet to the leg that dropped him to one knee, but nevertheless managed to take out a third terrorist.

Jana and Bledshaw each got one, but the last terrorist, screaming with rage, flicked his assault rifle to the full auto and sprayed the area.

Major Singh took one to the shoulder, slammed against the wall, and fell. Bledshaw clamped his side. Jacob and Jana filled the last man with bullets.

As quickly as it started, it was over. Silence fell over the room. Jacob sprang to his feet and ran around the bank of electronic controls to check for more threats. No other terrorists.

He circled around just in time to see the two sentries from upstairs rushing down. One fired at him. Jacob ducked and the bullet panged off the console with a shower of sparks. Bledshaw shot one through the chest and he tumbled down the stairs. Major Singh, despite having been shot twice, traded rounds with the other sentry and took him out.

Bledshaw ran for the controls. "I hope that shot didn't destroy the mechanism!"

"You're bleeding!"

"Nicked me. I'm fine."

"I'll guard the stairway," Jacob said, scooping up an assault rifle from a dead terrorist. "Jana, can you help the major?"

"Help Private Upadhyaya. He is still alive!" the major said, pointing at one of his men. He lay gasping on the ground, mouth bubbling with blood from a shot to the lung. The other man was obviously dead, a head shot having taken off a portion of his skull the size of a baseball.

Jacob got to the foot of the stairs and covered it. He heard shouts in Hindi and running feet. Major Singh crawled over to Jacob's position, leaving a pair of bloody trails.

"Take it easy, major."

"I must speak with my men. If they are not terrorists, I do not want any unnecessary bloodshed."

The guy looked so woozy, Jacob hoped that conversation would come soon. He didn't have long before he passed out.

"The keypad isn't working!" Bledshaw shouted. "I think that shot clipped a wire."

"Maybe I can fix it," Jacob said. He glanced over at Jana, who was helping the wounded private as much as she could. She always carried a small medical pack and was stuffing gauze into the wound. The internal hemorrhaging would be the real danger, though. The man needed a hospital, and soon.

"I can get it," Bradshaw said. He ran over to a toolkit sitting on the floor.

You're an electrician too?

Before he could actually ask that question, a shout came from upstairs. Jacob readied his weapon.

Major Singh put a bloody hand on the barrel.

"I think they're OK." Then he shouted something in Hindi and got a nervous reply. The conversation went back and forth for a moment before the major translated. "They are holding off and sending for a medic."

Jacob spared a glance at Bledshaw, who had unscrewed the casing in record time and was now fiddling with some wires.

"Got it!" Bledshaw said.

"Got what?" the major asked.

"There's a hidden room underneath this level," Jacob told him. "We think that's where the charges are planted."

"Director Rao never told me that."

"Director Rao didn't know. It's top secret."

"My government should have informed us!"

Jacob didn't reply. What was there to say?

He heard a series of electronic beeps as Bledshaw punched in the code, and a portion of the floor rose up like a hatch to reveal a narrow, hidden stairway. Major Singh drew in a sharp breath.

Gunfire erupted on the level above, punctuated by shouts of surprise and anguish.

"More traitors!" the major shouted, pulling out his pistol with his one good arm. Jacob got ready.

"I'll go down and check the storage room," Bledshaw said.

Jana sprang to her feet. "I'll go with you. There's nothing more I can do for the private."

Good. I don't trust that guy alone.

Just as Bledshaw and Jana disappeared down the stairs, a pair of soldiers appeared at the top of the upper level and poured fire down on him and the major.

CHAPTER FIFTEEN

Jana had to hurry to keep up with Bledshaw, who pelted down a narrow flight of metal stairs with a familiarity that told her he had been here before.

But how could he have been? How could the Antiquities Division access these hidden chambers without the dam staff knowing?

That question got swept away as she reached the bottom of the stairs and got stopped short by a breathtaking sight.

A large room filled with shelves of stunning artifacts.

They were all of the Mauryan period—elaborate temple friezes and pillars topped with sculptures of lions. Statues of deities and stunning gold jewelry with rubies and emeralds that gleamed in the harsh florescent light.

One shelf especially attracted her eye. On it was a row of ancient jars with copper wires attached to their lids. The lids were sealed with bitumen. Next to them was something that looked like a primitive dynamo. Next to that sat a painted wooden tablet with a detailed map of the heavens.

Then there were the inscriptions, shelf upon shelf of inscriptions in a language she couldn't read but which she suspected held great secrets of this ancient civilization, secrets that proved the Mauryan Empire to be even more advanced than anyone had ever suspected.

Her sense of wonder was quickly replaced with anger. These artifacts belonged in a museum where people could study them. Didn't scholars have a right to access all information from the past in order to make a clear picture of bygone ages? Didn't the people of India have a right to know the true extent of their ancestors' accomplishments? Didn't the whole world have a right to this heritage?

Jana spotted Bledshaw by the far wall, and her anger was replaced by terror.

For sunk into the floor were several shafts capped with detonators, just like in the Harper Dam. They were connected by dozens of intertwined wires to a timer resting against the wall.

Jana hurried over.

"Look," Bledshaw said, pointing a trembling finger. "They told us we have hours, but the timer says we have barely ten minutes."

"Can't we disconnect it?"

"Not the way this is wired. We try to do that, and it will go off immediately."

Jana didn't ask how he knew that. Bledshaw obviously had several skills he hadn't bothered to tell them.

"Can you disarm it?"

"Maybe." He clunked down the toolkit he had brought with him and rummaged around inside.

"Are you all right?"

The blood had soaked the side of his jacket, and a grim red rivulet was spreading down his pants leg.

"Considerably better than I'll be if I don't disarm this bomb. Get up there and warn the Indians that they need to evacuate immediately."

"No way they can evacuate the city in time!"

"No, but a few might get away."

Gunfire echoed down from upstairs.

"We're trapped. The terrorists and Jacob are still fighting."

"Then break through!" Bledshaw snapped.

Jana rushed upstairs to find Jacob and Major Singh still at the bottom of the stairs, trading shots with the terrorists who blocked the only exit. Major Singh lay on the floor and looked about to faint from blood loss. Still, he managed to peek around the corner of the stairwell and fire shots upstairs.

Jana grabbed an assault rifle from one of the dead bodies, snapped in a fresh magazine, and went to join them.

"Bledshaw's found the bomb," she shouted over the din. "We need to warn everybody."

"They got us pinned down," Jacob said, ducking back moments before a three-round burst chewed up the concrete next to him.

"We need to get through somehow. The bomb is going to blow in ten minutes. A warning won't help the city of Patna, but some people in the villages along the river might get away. We might save thousands of lives."

While hundreds of thousands more will die.

Or millions? Would it really wipe out the whole urban area?

Jana tried not to think about that. If she did, terror might paralyze her.

Jacob fired a burst around the stairwell. Sitting out of the line of fire, his leg and shoulder bleeding freely, Major Singh ejected the magazine from his pistol and fumbled to get a new one in. He dropped it, nearly toppled over as he picked it up from the floor and snapped it in.

"We can't get up there," Jacob said. "They got good cover and so do we. We haven't hit anyone for a couple of minutes now."

Jana had seen this before, both sides popping out of cover to trade shots. It could last for ages.

They didn't even have ten minutes.

They heard gunshots further away. It sounded like the terrorists were holding the upper floor while loyalists among the Indian regiment were trying to rub them out from the floor above. Just one floor of evil between them and the chance to save thousands of lives.

"We got to change the game somehow," Jana said.

Major Singh leaned against the wall and slowly pushed himself up on his one good leg.

"How?" Jacob said, sending a few more ineffective bullets up the stairs and getting some in return. "Rushing them would be suicide."

With a roar and a shouted phrase in Punjabi, Major Singh rushed past them, limping precariously, and stumbled up the stairs, firing as he went.

He didn't make it three steps before bullets tore through his beefy frame and he toppled back.

But he had given Jacob and Jana the chance they needed. Both men at the top of the stairs had exposed themselves. One was tumbling down the steps, hit by Major Singh's last shot.

The other one went down in a flurry of bullets as Jana and Jacob leaped over the heroic major's corpse and rushed up the stairs.

Another terrorist appeared around the corner. He never got a chance to fire before he jerked and fell with three gunshot wounds to the chest. Jana and Jacob leapt over his body too.

They peeked around the corner of the engineering room and saw three more soldiers all firing up the next set of stairs. A few bodies were clustered around both sets of stairs. The terrorists had been taking casualties from the CIA and their former colleagues.

They must have known that taking such an isolated position against overwhelming odds would mean their deaths, and yet they had done so anyway, simply to delay any rescue operations.

These people were sacrificing their own lives in order to kill hundreds of thousands of others.

Not on her watch. Jana leveled her assault rifle and along with Jacob cut down the three survivors.

They hurried over to the other staircase. Jana threw her gun into view of the men upstairs and put both empty hands out around the corner.

"We got them, but there's a bomb and it's going to blow in ten minutes!"

All she got back was a babble of suspicious Hindi.

Of all the times to face a language barrier!

She drew in a breath, squared her shoulders, and stepped into view.

A couple of terrified faces, and terrifying assault rifle muzzles, faced her. They demanded something in Hindi. She tried to take a step up the stairs, and they made a threatening motion.

"The bomb!" she shouted. "The bomb goes off in ten minutes."

How frustrating! She felt like a tourist speaking loud, slow English, assuming everyone in the world would understand her.

A sergeant appeared, leveling his assault rifle at her.

"What did you say about the bomb?" he asked in English.

"We've found it. It's set to go off in ten minutes."

"Who else is with you?"

"Only my two CIA companions. Private Upadhyaya is seriously injured. The rest of us and the terrorists are dead."

"The other two show themselves."

Jacob set down his gun and came out with his hands up.

"Where is the third American?"

"He's trying to defuse the bomb. He's on a lower level."

The sergeant gave them a suspicious scowl. Jana squirmed with impatience but couldn't blame him. He'd just lost comrades to the treachery of people in his own regiment.

"Don't move," he ordered.

The three of them came down, quickly followed by five more. They shoved Jana and Jacob up against the wall and patted them down. Major Singh lay at their feet. Jana looked at him sadly. He'd been a true hero. If they got out of this, she'd push for him to get India's highest honor.

The soldiers finished searching then and then surveyed the carnage in the engineering room, eyes wide.

"Two levels down," Jana said.

“There is only one more level,” the sergeant said.

“There are two, the one you know and a secret one. We need to hurry.”

The sergeant jerked his head, and they rushed to the staircase. The soldiers made a ring around them and kept them covered as they went downstairs and beheld the secret doorway open in the floor.

The sergeant gasped out something in Hindi and led them down.

Bledshaw was still there, looking pale, the bloodstain having spread to cover his entire pants leg. He was still tinkering with the electronics. The timer said eight minutes.

To his credit, the sergeant didn't skip a beat. He whipped out a walkie-talkie and rushed upstairs to get a signal.

Jacob stepped forward. “How’s it going?”

“I … ” Sweat beaded on Bledshaw’s forehead. “This is more complicated than I thought.”

“Let me help you. I’ve been trained for this.” Jacob came up and started examining the timer.

“Can you do it?” Jana whispered.

Jacob didn’t reply except for a tiny shake of the head. Jana got the impression that he didn’t even know that he was doing it.

An unconscious admission that he didn’t know what to do.

CHAPTER SIXTEEN

Patrol officer Anil Mishra of the Patna Police Force was witnessing utter chaos.

When the terrorists who blew up the American dam released their statement, the chief had dusted off an old evacuation plan and briefed everyone in all the precincts. Everyone had agreed that it seemed a wise precaution, and everyone had agreed that given the thousands of dams around the world, that was all it was—a precaution. Something to soothe the politicians and keep the more outspoken and panicky members of the public quiet.

Officer Mishra had looked up the number of hydroelectric dams in India and found there were nearly two hundred. So even if the group targeted India next, and he saw no reason why they would, the odds that Patna would be hit were still small.

And yet it had happened, and that dusty old evacuation plan dating to a time of tension with Pakistan ten years ago was proving totally unmanageable.

Officer Mishra stood at an intersection, trying to keep the traffic moving. His every instinct screamed at him to run, but he knew if he did so, he could never live with himself. His father had been a policeman, as had his grandfather under the English in the last days of the Raj. They had both served with honor. Anil would not betray the Mishra family name.

This was a main street that ran through town and after a couple of miles led to the highway leading out of the city. The street was clogged with trucks, cars, taxis, motorcycles, and pedestrians, taking up all four lanes and heading all in one direction, pushing aside the traffic that had been going into town rather than out of it.

Five minutes ago, the street had been normal. Busy but not unmanageable. Now that news of the bomb had gone over the radio, TV, and Internet, the entire city seemed to be out here.

He had no backup and had switched off his radio because it was filled with frantic officers speaking over one another.

Finding himself alone on duty, Mishra had ordered a some fruit vendors from a nearby open-air market to block the side streets with their carts. He wanted to keep the traffic flowing on the main street. The problem was, panicked residents coming up those side streets wanted to get on the main road and sent up a cacophony of blaring horns. When the fruit sellers didn't move their carts, either because they wanted to obey police orders or had already fled themselves, they started shoving the carts to the side. One idiot rammed his car into a cart of melons, overturning it and spilling the melons onto the main street, where they were soon mashed to a pulp. The car nosed its way in, blocking two lanes of traffic.

Officer Mishra blew on his whistle so hard he thought his head would burst. The driver ignored him and pulled into the center lane, smacking the car ahead of him. That began a shouting match between the two drivers.

That slowed things down even more. The pedestrians filing past were going faster than the vehicles now.

The sound of another fender bender made him look at the other side of the four-lane road. A city bus coming off another side street Officer Mishra had tried to block had knocked aside a pair of carts and was grinding its way through traffic, the driver using the bigger size of his vehicle to force the cars to give way.

The police officer ran between the cars, edging their way forward, blowing his whistle and waving his hands at the driver, a municipal employee who should have known better. The driver ignored him. Everyone was ignoring him in their urge to get out of the city.

How long did they have? The alert hadn't said, only saying that everyone should leave the city immediately.

As if that were possible! It would take a couple of days to get everyone out of Patna and up to high ground. The terrorists couldn't have offered them days. It would be minutes.

Minutes? No one would get out.

He had no idea how much the city would flood. No one did. The government hadn't mentioned that, at least not to people on his junior level. Indeed, beyond the bus he was frantically waving at, he could see a restaurant full of people, the lunch crowd staring curiously out the window as if they were seeing something interesting on television rather than the worst mass panic in Patna's history. Some fools weren't taking the warnings seriously at all.

At least they will die in peace.

Unlike me.

The bus kept shoving cars out of the way, metal screeched and people swore. Officer Mishra had to vault over the hood of a car as the space closed up in front of him.

At last he got in front of the bus and stopped it by standing in its path, making angry eye contact with the driver, and putting a hand on his gun.

The driver jerked to a stop, shaking his fist. Passengers crowded around the front window to shout at the policeman.

The screech of metal and a chorus of screams made Officer Mishra look to the opposite side of the street. The cars pushed aside by the bus were still crowding to that side, one hitting another and that one hitting another. That whole section of the traffic jam shifted and the panicked driver at the far side, avoiding the tide of metal, swerved onto the sidewalk.

Straight into the teeming crowd.

Officer Mishra saw a woman go under the wheels. Another pedestrian got his foot run over. Others banged on the hood of the car. One guy started kicking the driver's side door.

Within seconds, a small riot flared up around the car. Office Mishra had to walk over several tightly packed cars to get there. He started pulling angry pedestrians away from the car.

"Help the woman!" he shouted. "Stop fighting and help the casualties."

The crowd swirled around the stalled vehicle. The screams of pain and terror had acted like an electric charge on the masses and now they rushed along the sidewalk, rushing they knew not where, only away.

Officer Mishra stumbled and tried to check the tide. The press of humanity moved him along like a leaf in a river. It was all he could do to stay upright. He saw one old man go down and disappear in a forest of trampling feet. Then another person went down. And a third, a teenage girl, quite close to him.

Office Mishra reached out for her, got knocked off balance, and fell hard on the pavement. He cried out as someone stepped on his hand, the sound cut off and strangled as another foot trod on his neck.

And then he was flat on his back, pain all over his body as countless feet crushed him. Blearily, he saw the girl he had tried to save getting trampled just a few feet away.

They don't need to blow up the dam, was Officer Mishra's last thought. *They are already destroying the city.*

***

Jacob looked at the bomb timer and saw that it was nearly covered in a mass of wires going every which way. Bledshaw had already clipped and removed several false leads, but there were a few more wires so tucked into the network that he couldn't tell if any particular one would stop the timer or set it off.

Jacob couldn't tell either. Bledshaw was obviously good at this, but not good enough to defuse this bomb.

Jacob wasn't sure he was good enough either.

Don't freeze. Don't freeze. Do. Not. Freeze.

That moment in Ljubljana when he stared down the barrel of a pistol and let their one suspect get away flashed through his mind's eye.

He had failed. He had choked, and he failed.

Don't fail again. An entire city is relying on you.

An entire country. If Patna got wiped out, the shock would shatter India's economy. It would spiral into a deep depression, millions would lose work and India's poor, always teetering on the edge, would face starvation.

The world's largest democracy, with its expanding economy and booming tech industry, would become the world's basket case.

He looked at the wires again. Bledshaw's hand hovered over them with the wire cutters, unsure what to do next.

"I think that red wire is a decoy," Jacob said. "See the way it loops around the green one to hide where it's going? That's to make us suspect it."

"But it could do that to hide the fact that it's a trap."

Jacob nodded. "It could at that."

"What about the other red wire?"

"Not sure. Could defuse it, could set it off."

"You can't decide?" Bledshaw sounded pained. The timer had just gone past two minutes.

"Fifty-fifty."

Bledshaw gently moved the wires around as much as their tight mass would allow, trying to trace where they went.

"This blue one is a decoy," Bledshaw said.

Jacob opened his mouth to object. He thought it was a trap.

Bledshaw clipped it and Jacob clenched his teeth, waiting to get blown to atoms.

Nothing happened. He let out a breath.

“You’re not half bad,” Jacob gasped.

Bledshaw removed the wire, and they could see a bit better. A green wire was an obvious decoy, and he clipped it away. It didn't give them a better view of the remaining wires.

Bledshaw paused again. One minute and twenty seconds.

“Now what?” he asked, sounding as helpless as Jacob felt.

“I … I think that white one sets it off.”

Bledshaw pried around the wires, trying to get a better view. He couldn’t.

"I think the last red one is the one to shut it off. But I can't see for sure unless I get this yellow one, and I'm not sure about that one."

“I’m pretty sure it’s a decoy. The pattern of wires looks similar to a bomb I defused before.”

“You’re pretty sure it’s a decoy?”

“Yeah.”

“*Pretty* sure?”

The clock went below one minute.

Jacob shrugged. “That’s all I got.”

“We have to risk it.”

Jacob winced as he cut the yellow wire. Nothing happened.

Bledshaw stripped the wire away and let out a cry of triumph.

They could now see that the red wire was obviously a trap, which meant either the white wire or the orange one turned off the timer. Neither looked like a trap, but Jacob couldn't say that for sure.

“Which one?” Bledshaw whispered.

“Dunno.”

The clock went below thirty seconds.

“Well, *guess*.”

“Cut the orange.”

He did. Nothing happened.

“The white! Cut the white!”

Bledshaw cut the white.

The timer didn’t stop.

"What? How?" Bledshaw cried. There was only the lone red wire left, and with all the others stripped away, it was clear that it was a trap.

“I don’t know. I’ve never seen this before.”

“Should I cut—”

“No!”

“But—”

“There’s got to be something we’re missing.”

"But what?"

They stared at the timer. Jacob didn't see any solution. He glanced over at the charges in their large holes bored into the floor and gasped as he realized the truth.

This wasn't the timer. This was a decoy. The timer was in one of those boreholes.

But which one?

He ran over and looked at them. Just like with the fake timer, there was a mass of wires connecting the charges to each other. He started going through them one by one, looking for extra wires. The borehole with one more wire than the others would be the one with the timer.

He glanced over at the fake timer. Ten seconds. Did that matter? Was that even the real time they had left?

"Jacob … " Bledshaw's voice came out pained.

"I know, I know."

Bingo! The only one with an extra wire. Using a screwdriver, he gently pulled the cap off the charge a couple of millimeters and saw that instead of a borehole filled with explosives, there was an empty hole lit by the glow of an LED display.

He pulled it up.

"Ah!" Bledshaw cried. Jacob glanced over and saw the timer had run to zero.

And yet they were still here.

He looked down at the other timer and found it had also gone down to zero.

He also saw that the wires didn't actually connect the timer to the charges. Jacob traced them to the next borehole, pried it up, and saw the hole was filled with simple putty, not C4 or dynamite.

He checked the rest and found the same thing.

The entire bomb plot had been a ruse.

***

Thousands of miles away in Turkey, the Turkish troops were on high alert. Every dam was being protected by at least one regiment. The air force had established a no-fly zone within ten miles of any dam, and the police had rounded up anyone with known connections to radical groups or arms smugglers.

They were doing what so many other nations were doing—scrambling all their available forces to protect their infrastructure.

Like with Patna, the efforts were in vain.

The Gulumkale hydroelectric dam in the southwestern part of the country suddenly exploded, the force of the shock and the collapsing span of concrete so great that people felt the tremor a hundred miles away. While there was no large city downstream, the rich farmland on either side of the river was dotted with villages and towns.

All of these were swept away. Fifty thousand people drowned in a matter of minutes.

CHAPTER SEVENTEEN

Aaron Peters felt much better now that he was back in the game. He only wished he knew what the hell this game was all about.

Luckily he knew someone who could answer that for him, which is why he had taken a flight to Toronto as fast as he could.

Canadians are often stereotyped as affable, self-effacing, and maybe a little bit weak, citizens of a pleasant country that never gets in the news because nothing dramatic ever happens there.

Whatever the truth may or may not be behind those stereotypes, they didn't apply to Darren Altbridge.

Darren was a career criminal with a very profitable and very dangerous specialty—snitching.

This isn't the kind of thing that will get you thrown in prison, but it could get you carved up and fed to dogs by the cartels, the victim of a drive-by shooting by street gangs, or getting bludgeoned to death by your everyday common criminal.

On the other hand, being a snitch could be highly lucrative. There wasn't much competition thanks to the danger and the strict code of not talking to the law most in the underworld adhered to, so there was a high demand for Darren Altbridge's services.

How he discovered his information was a mystery. Like with a similar contact in Italy that Jacob had used recently, no one really knew how he did it, just that his information was always accurate. He never lied to a client and wouldn't accept payment if he didn't know the answer to a question.

Aaron had a thick envelope of CIA slush funds in the pocket of his blazer. He hoped he'd get to spend it. So far, all his contacts had shrugged their shoulders and professed ignorance of anyone named Robert Bledshaw or an organization called the Antiquities Division. That bothered him. He'd questioned a cross-section of the best-informed men and women in the Western world.

Darren Altman was his last chance.

A taxi took Aaron through downtown Toronto, prosperous and at peace, or at least superficially so. The West, indeed the whole world, was in constant danger of falling apart. Terrorism, a rising tide of extremism and intolerance, environmental and population problems, and the unsustainability of an overheated economic system. So many factors that could bring it all crashing down.

You wouldn't know it from all those apathetic faces he passed, sipping their lattes and staring at their phones. A prickling sense of unease kept him tense. He didn't fit in here in the West. He couldn't be so relaxed, couldn't care more about Tiktok than geopolitics. Couldn't live a life of ignorant bliss.

He felt more at home in Afghanistan. There, the people lived life close to the bone. Life was a daily struggle for survival, and if most of the Afghanis' problems were self-made thanks to their incessant tribal feuding, at least they weren't like the sleepwalkers he saw here in Toronto, or New York, or London, or any prosperous place in the West.

He'd been shielded from this feeling while in his lakeside cabin in Maine. Wallace had been smart to send him there—all the luxuries of the West without any of the stressors. He had enjoyed central heating and running water while not having to deal with the passivity of a people who didn't know how precarious their prosperity was, and through such ignorance risked losing it all.

Aaron tried to ignore the bright shops and glittering office buildings and the soaring CN Tower that dominated Toronto's skyline and focus on the mission. If Altman could give him some intel, he could get to work. If not, he wasn't sure what his next move would be.

A detail on the sidewalk outside made him perk up. A young man, barely in his twenties, was staring at his phone with a look of shock. Obviously not staring at Tiktok. Then he saw a middle-aged woman who was also staring at her phone, her mouth a horrified O. She nudged her husband and made him look. His brow furrowed with concern.

Aaron got on his phone and found all the news sites lit up with banner headlines.

A dam in Turkey had been hit. The ensuing flood had wiped out several towns and the entire countryside downriver.

God, I hope Jana and Jacob weren't there.

He sent a quick text to them both, then fidgeted in the back seat of the taxi, waiting for a reply. Aaron found himself scrolling through the vague initial reports of the disaster. What the hell did the Antiquities Division have in these dams that was so important?

"Here we are," the taxi driver said, pulling off into the parking lot of a park along the shore of Lake Ontario.

Aaron paid and stepped out into the crisp northern air. He walked along a narrow path through the green park and past a bubbling fountain. It was a weekday and so the park was quiet, only a few joggers and elderly dog walkers. Altman liked meeting in public places but not too public. Aaron kept alert. People like Altman always attracted trouble. Considering some of the people he'd crossed, it was a miracle the guy was still breathing.

The terrain gently sloped down to the lakeside. A cool breeze blew in from over the water. A path ran alongside with a few joggers and people lazing about on park benches. It all seemed so peaceful. Didn't these people know the world was tearing itself apart?

No, they didn't, not even if they read about the dam attacks. They would read such news with horror, shake their heads, and go on with their ordinary lives as if none of it could ever touch them. That was the blessing, and the curse, that Aaron's work gave them.

He spotted Altman leaning against the railing of the waterside walkway, his back to the lake and facing the park and path. Always alert. Like an Afghani. Like a CIA agent. Like anyone in the game.

Altman was a short, stocky man in his early forties with a blonde buzzcut and closely set blue eyes that always remained in motion. He wore a loose windbreaker to cover up what Aaron was sure would be a shoulder holster. Concealed carry was illegal in Canada, but Altman wouldn't care. The law was the least of his worries.

Aaron wished he had a gun of his own. He hadn't had time to arrange it with the local CIA fixer. He hadn't even contacted them. The Order might still have its tentacles deep in the CIA, and he didn't want his movements to be known.

As he approached the snitch, Aaron made a quick situational analysis. An elderly couple sat at a nearby park bench, gazing out at the lake and holding hands. A young woman who was obviously a professional dog walker stood a few yards away next to a bush as half a dozen dogs on leashes sniffed and peed. They were every breed from Doberman to Chihuahua. In the distance, a couple of young men jogged toward them.

Aaron walked over to Altman, who shook his hand.

"Good to see you again, Kevin," Altman said, using one of Aaron's aliases. Altman didn't know his real name, not that he'd ever reveal it to anyone else. He only snitched on criminals. To snitch on the CIA would be suicidal.

"How are things, Darren?"

He shrugged, still looking around. “Can’t complain.”

Aaron leaned against the railing, too. "You seen the news, I suppose.”

“Of course. What the hell is going on?”

“I was hoping you’d tell me.”

“Terrorism is a bit outside my wheelhouse.”

“Ever hear of the Antiquities Division?”

Altman’s eyes sparked with surprise, but his demeanor remained unchanged.

“That’s a name I don’t hear much.”

Hope rose in Aaron’s heart. “So you’ve heard of them?”

“Sure. Don’t know much but … ”

Altman’s voice trailed off as he focused on something to their left. Aaron gave a glance and only saw the two young joggers.

Wait. Something was off about those two joggers.

They looked a bit too intent, a bit too in sync, a bit too alert to be gym bros. They weren’t wearing ear buds like everyone under thirty, and now that they had drawn closer Aaron could see their calloused knuckles.

Altman reached into his windbreaker.

Just then, a rush of air and a soft patter tore their attention from the joggers.

The dog walker had released the Doberman, and it was charging at them, teeth bared. It didn't bark or growl, just charged. Well trained. Altman drew his pistol just as the huge dog leaped and clamped its teeth around the snitch's wrist.

The gun went off, the report loud in the peaceful park. The two joggers reached into the waistbands of their gym shorts, and each brought out a telescoping baton. They snapped them open and bore down on Altman and Aaron.

As his contact struggled with the dog, Aaron charged the two joggers. Just as they came at him, one swinging high and one low, Aaron dropped to the ground, rolled under the low swing, and slammed a fist into a vulnerable crotch.

The man doubled over with a grunt. Aaron lashed out at his pal, trying to kick the guy’s kneecap, but he dodged nimbly to the side and swept down with his baton. Aaron rolled away an instant before the metal rod, with its deadly knob at the end, smacked on the sidewalk so hard it chipped the concrete.

Aaron kept rolling as the man chased him, swinging the baton in bone-crushing arcs.

Another shot rang out. Unfortunately, it wasn't at the guy threatening him. Another swing, and Aaron risked leaping to his feet.

In the half-second it took to do so, the guy got ready and swung again. Aaron had no choice but to close. There was no time to dodge. He grunted as the shaft slammed into his shoulder. At least he didn't get hit with the knob. He grappled with the jogger, who jabbed the butt of the handle into his back, aiming for his kidney but thankfully missing.

Aaron grabbed his opponent's free hand, twisted, and got him into an armlock. Then he slammed the guy's face into the railing. The first time wasn't enough to make him drop the weapon so he did it again, and a third time.

The jogger collapsed in a heap at Aaron's feet.

Just in time to be replaced by his red-faced companion. Aaron had to hand it to him. After a crotch punch like that, most guys would be singing soprano for a good ten minutes, but here he was wanting to get back in fight after just a few seconds.

Aaron barely dodged a swing from the baton, ducking to his left to move away from the railing and get more room to maneuver. The guy came in slowly and with care, baton poised, fist clenched to strike or block. Aaron tried a kick, barely got away with his leg intact, and circled around. Vaguely, he could hear screams, perhaps from the old couple. Someone would surely have called the police by now.

The jogger swung at his face. Aaron leapt back, then had to retreat further when the backhand came swinging hard at his neck.

This guy was good, and the ache in Aaron's shoulder and back from his friend's strikes weren't helping Aaron get any moves in. It was all he could do to dodge the attacks.

Then Altman came to the rescue with a kick to the small of the jogger's back.

He stumbled forward, let down his guard, and Aaron needed no further invitation. He dove in, dealt a karate chop to the wrist that would have broken the bones of a lesser man but at least made him drop that damn baton, then a strike to the bridge of the nose that took him down.

"Grandpa over there called the cops," Altman said. "We got to get out of here."

Aaron looked around. Both joggers were still down and the dog walker had vanished, leaving a bunch of confused looking pooches standing around by the bushes. The Doberman treaded water in the lake.

"Did you hurt the dog?" Aaron asked.

"I just threw him in the lake. I should have shot him. Look what he did to me!" Altman held up his arm. His cuff was torn to shreds, and his wrist bled freely.

Aaron smacked him upside the head. "I like dogs!"

"So do I when they're not trying to eat me. Now let's get the hell out of here."

Aaron smacked him upside the head again as they ran off into a forested area of the park. Altman stopped in a sheltered area and turned his windbreaker inside out, revealing bright red cloth instead of drab khaki. Then he put on a Toronto Blue Jays cap and a pair of what looked like prescription glasses. Aaron took a second look and saw the lenses were flat, not corrective at all.

"That should fool the pigs," Altman said. "Aren't you going to change?"

"No. If they come for us, I'll just point to you and run."

"Very funny."

They started to walk, looking all around them. No sign of the police. Aaron figured they had at least a couple of minutes. They stuck to the overgrown part of the park.

"Who were those guys?" Aaron asked.

"None of your concern."

"My bruises are very much my concern."

"Some cocaine dealers sent them. At least I think so. Could have been that human trafficking gang. Or it might have been—"

"Never mind. Tell me what you know about the Antiquities Division."

Altman cocked his head, eyes glittering with greed. "How much is it worth to you?"

Aaron pulled out the envelope of cash and slapped Altman with it.

"That's for the dog."

"Hey! You're lucky you're CIA or I'd flatten you."

Aaron snorted. Actually, it wasn't entirely a boast. Altman could handle himself. He wouldn't still be alive if he couldn't.

"I'd like to see you try. Now tell me what you know."

A siren wailed in the distance behind them. It sounded pretty far off. Nevertheless, they picked up the pace. Altman pocketed the envelope, looked around to make sure no one was looking, and said,

"What I heard made no sense. I didn't believe it at the time, and I'm not sure I believe it now."

"Tell me anyway."

"The only reason I think it might be true is that you're asking. They're tied up in these dam attacks, aren't they?"

"I'm asking the questions you're answering."

Altman gave another nervous look around, and Aaron could tell it wasn't because of the police sirens.

"Well, you're not going to believe this but … "

Altman then told a tale that was so outlandish, so unbelievable, that in any other situation Aaron would have dismissed it out of hand.

But Altman was right. The Antiquities Division's connection to the dam attacks made him take it seriously.

And by taking it seriously, he had to question everything else he had always assumed to be true.

He immediately thought of Jana. When his daughter heard this, it was going to destroy her world.

CHAPTER EIGHTEEN

Jacob looked down at the rushing waters coming through the penstock of the Patna Dam and felt more miserable than he ever had.

The terrorists had tricked them. They had lured them here through a false lead they knew he and Jana would follow while they set off the real bomb in Turkey.

It had been a masterful act of deception, requiring an intimate knowledge of their adversaries. Whoever had led them on had known Bledshaw would have revealed the contents of the Harper Dam to them, that Jana would have found the connection to the Mauryan artifacts, that Bledshaw would have seen the importance of the connection and taken them here. They had also known that Jacob would have trusted Jana's instincts and would have agreed to follow the lead.

So the enemy knew that Bledshaw had recruited them, and knew just how each of them would think.

Who the hell were these people?

More than a deception, this had been a trap. The terrorists who they had recruited from within the Indian Army regiment hadn't been there to defend the bomb in order for it to go off. The soldiers might have thought that, but in reality, they had been there to assassinate himself, Jana, and Bledshaw. The bomb had been nothing but a ruse.

But that led to a strange conclusion—they had chosen a dam that would cause far fewer casualties when it burst than the Patna Dam. Initial reports stated that the Gulumkale hydroelectric dam explosion had led to 50,000 people being declared missing. That was simply government damage control. Almost all of them would have been killed. But hitting Patna Dam would have killed hundreds of thousands, perhaps millions, so why not go for the bigger death toll? Why go through all the trouble of recruiting soldiers for a suicide mission, plant a fake bomb when you could have just as easily planted a real one, and then do a second, equally complex mission elsewhere in order to blow up an entirely different dam?

Plus, a bomb at Patna Dam would have had a far greater chance of killing Jacob and his companions than the soldiers had. The terrorists knew enough about him to know that. So why the double attack? Were they trying to minimize casualties? Or was there another reason?

He turned and surveyed the top of the dam, which now teemed with police officers in riot gear, plus a number of plainclothes detectives. The police had been brought in to take over from the soldiers, who were now suspect. The air force still circled overhead, but the army had been moved out of range.

Bledshaw sat at the back of an ambulance not far off in what must have been a very uncomfortable conversation for him—trying to explain to the Patna chief of police how he knew about a secret room full of priceless artifacts hidden in the dam. A medic was patching Bledshaw's side, but that provoked not a shred of sympathy in the chief of police, who looked like he was ripping the director of the Antiquities Division a new one.

Good. He deserved it. He'd been bullshitting them this entire time, and now he looked like he was trying bullshit the Patna chief of police, talking a mile a minute when he could get a word in edgewise.

Where was Jana? She must still be downstairs with the artifacts, assuming the police hadn't kicked her out. A bomb disposal team had gone down there and confirmed the charges were all duds. An announcement had gone out to the public that Patna was now safe, although one of the cops had told him there was chaos in the city, with several hundred people killed or injured from being trampled or run over.

What a mess. If Bledshaw had been a bit more forthcoming, this all might have been avoided.

Or maybe not. He'd been fooled just as much as everybody else.

He checked his phone. No communications from Aaron. The satellite phone was back at the plane. He'd need to call in to Tyler Wallace and find out what the CIA had found out, if anything.

Jacob took a deep breath and went to a news site, knowing and dreading what he would see.

And there it was. A Turkish valley, once full of towns and villages, now ravaged by the flood. The flood waters were now receding, the initial rush having passed and the water level gradually lowering to what it once was. Jacob scrolled through horrid images of concrete buildings cracked like walnuts, large dismembered sections scattered downriver. Corpses of people and animals floated in the water or lay covered in mud on the banks. In one shot, a hill above a town was covered in a sad cluster of refugees, surrounded by swirling waters filled with the bodies of their friends and neighbors.

Jacob put away his phone, heartsick. He went downstairs to check on Jana. None of the police stopped them. The CIA agents had killed the traitors and stopped the bomb. They had proven they were no threat.

But they had also proven they couldn't be trusted. A pair of policemen, both high-ranking officers toting machineguns, dogged his footsteps.

He passed down through the two lower levels and the carnage within. He stopped short when he saw a pair of medics treating one of the turncoat soldiers, who lay groaning on the ground.

A prisoner! That might just give them the clues they needed.

"Will he live?" Jacob asked.

His police escort gave him an uncomprehending stare. One of the medics looked up and said, "He is a serious case. A bullet cut his spine and he is paralyzed from the chest down. He also has internal bleeding. We must stabilize him before we risk taking him up the stairs, but I think he will pull through."

"Did any of the other terrorists live?"

"One did for a time, but he has since died."

"Take care of this guy. He might be a key witness."

The medic frowned. "I know that. Do you think I am stupid?"

"No. It's just … it's been a bad day."

The medic nodded, his face softening. "No problem."

The medic got back to work, only to get interrupted by a barked question from one of the two policemen standing close behind Jacob, who obviously wanted an account of what had just been said.

I hope they don't try and stop us from leaving. We got work to do.

Where exactly?

Jacob continued to the secret hatch leading downstairs. He could hear Jana arguing with someone down there.

"I know this is your national heritage. I'm not trying to interfere. I'm only looking for evidence as to why it was targeted!"

"I said do not touch, madam."

"How can I get a good look at it if I don't move it?"

"Do you think this is an antique shop and you are a customer? *Do not touch*!"

It sounded like Jana's insatiable curiosity was getting her in trouble again. Jacob hurried down the stairs, the two cops close at his heels.

He found Jana standing close to a shelf of artifacts, arguing with a bespectacled older civilian with a bald patch and a gut. This unimposing figure was nevertheless standing his ground, fists on hips, keeping himself between Jana and the artifacts.

The man turned to Jacob as he appeared and treated him to an angry glare.

"Ah, another CIA operative who never informed us of our country's heritage being stolen!"

"I only found out about it yesterday," Jacob told him, he extended a hand. "Agent Snow at your service. And who might you be?"

The man did not shake the hand offered him.

"I am Professor Biswas, curator of the Patna Museum. I was called in when the police informed me of a room full of India's treasures hidden in a secret chamber only the CIA knew about!"

"Only some in the CIA," Jacob said, deciding not to blow Bledshaw's cover. "I and my associate here didn't know anything about it."

"And I am supposed to believe that!" Dr. Biswas scoffed.

Jacob decided to change course and hopefully defuse the situation. "Could you tell me the significance of these artifacts, doctor?"

"Groundbreaking! They changed all the history books, and the CIA had them hidden in one of our own dams. Why? Can you tell me that? Why?"

"I don't know the answers, professor. I work on a need-to-know basis."

"Well, I need to know what is going on here."

"Perhaps we can figure that out together," Jana said in a calm voice. "There seems to be a lot here of a technological level too far advanced for the time period."

Jana pointed to something that looked like a small grandfather clock. While battered and corroded, Jacob could see a complex mechanism of gears inside the crystal casing.

The professor, despite his anger, stared at it for a moment with awe.

"Amazing, isn't it?" he said in a hushed voice. "It looks like the Antikythera mechanism."

"It does," Jana agreed. "May I turn it around to see the other side?"

She took a step forward. The professor got in front of her. "I will."

He pulled out a pair of white gloves from his pocket, put them on, and with the care Jacob had seen Jana use with ancient objects gently picked it up and turned it around.

Jana and Dr. Biswas let out a gasp. They sounded so identical that Jacob had to smile.

On the other face of the clock thing was a brass dial with a bunch of notches on it along with words in some language Jacob didn't recognize, although it looked similar to what he saw on other inscriptions around the room.

"It really is an Antikythera mechanism!" Jana said.

"But with more functions," the professor said. "Look, this is for solar eclipses, and this is for lunar ones. And this calendar reaches back five thousand years! Why go back so far? Why backwards and not forwards?"

"Now that you two are getting along, care to tell me what an Antikythera mechanism is?" Jacob asked.

Jana said, "It was a device found in a shipwreck off the Greek island of Antikythera and dates to the second century BC, making it the world's oldest analog computer."

"This might be even older, considering the style of the Sanskrit inscriptions," the Indian professor said with obvious pride.

Jana nodded. "Yes, and like this example, the Antikythera mechanism could predict eclipses and other celestial phenomena. This one is even more important because it looks complete. The Antikythera mechanism was corroding at the bottom of the sea for two thousand years, and a lot of its parts are missing."

"This could revolutionize the history of science," Professor Biswas said, his eyes gleaming.

"It might even prove that the Mauryan Empire influenced the Greeks more than we thought," Jana agreed.

Jacob smiled. Their animosity of a few moments before seemed to have been forgotten thanks to their mutual scientific enthusiasm.

"So why would anyone want to destroy it?" Jacob asked.

"I don't know," Jana admitted. "But in fact, they didn't want to destroy it. They wanted to destroy whatever was in that Turkish dam."

Jacob bit his lip. Jana had just blundered.

Professor Biswas whirled on her. "What? There was another chamber of treasures in the dam in Turkey?"

"Perhaps. We don't know for sure," Jana said, blushing as she realized her mistake.

"There must have been! Why is the CIA hiding these things? You are not telling all you know."

Sad to say, we aren't hiding a thing. We're as much in the dark as you are, professor.

"More to the point, why is someone destroying them?" Jacob asked.

Jacob was beginning to formulate an idea. The Parthian and Mauryan collections had two things in common—rich treasures and examples of ancient technology. The rich treasures of gold and jewels, while impressive, were no big deal. If you wanted to destroy something like that, you could bomb the Smithsonian or the British Museum. No, the real distinction of these two collections was the ancient technology. In both cases, the collections contained items previously unknown to archaeologists.

Was the Antiquities Division hoarding evidence of ancient technology, and was this mysterious terrorist group trying to destroy it?

If so, why?

CHAPTER NINETEEN

It took some time to get herself away from Professor Biswas and pry Bledshaw away from the Patna chief of police, but once she did, Jana sat him down in a quiet section at the top of the dam, away from the crowds of policemen. The two officers who had been dogging Jacob's footsteps remained nearby, distracted by Jacob as he showed them the destruction in Turkey on his phone.

The two Indians looked drawn and sick as they looked at what could have happened to their own city.

"So what was in the dam in Turkey?" Jana asked.

"The Byzantine collection," Bledshaw said with a sigh. "Some really beautiful works of art."

"Were there any examples of ancient technology?" Jana asked.

Without realizing it, she and Jacob had come to the same conclusions.

"Yes. The Byzantines, as you no doubt know, inherited much of the knowledge of the ancient Classical cultures and made their own advances in medicine and steam power."

Jana nodded. There was a famous account in the medieval annals of the Byzantine emperor's throne being able to rise up to the ceiling and descend again, and of a golden tree in his garden with metal birds that sang. Scholars assumed these two devices had been powered by steam. The ancient Greeks had built smaller steam devices many centuries before, and Byzantium, as the last vestige of the Roman Empire, had always admired the ancient Greeks and spoke Greek as their native language.

"I'd like the see the database for that collection."

"Very well, if you think it can help."

Jacob strolled over. "What would help is if you level with us. Tens of thousands are dead, and these people are going to strike again. We need to plan our next move before they carry out theirs."

Bledshaw and Jana glanced at the two police officers, who stayed close.

"Don't worry about them," Jacob said. "I managed to figure out that they don't speak English. I watched them while an English-speaking newscaster said the bomb in Patna hadn't been defused and they didn't bat an eyelid."

"Why would a newscaster say that?" Jana asked.

"Journalists are always coming in late, and they're always getting it wrong. Now, Mr. Bledshaw, we need some answers from you."

Bledshaw looked at the ground, took a deep breath, and said, "We think the terrorist leader might be one of our own."

"Yeah, I kind of figured that since he knows about all your hiding places. What's his name?"

"Dr. Colin Harlow."

Jana gasped. "The archaeologist?"

"You know this guy?" Jacob asked.

"Yes. He was a leading archaeometallurgist, someone who specialized in the study of ancient metals. He was in high demand on excavations all around the world. He died in a car crash in Jordan ten years ago."

"No he didn't," Bledshaw said. "He faked his own death in order to devote his life to the Antiquities Division."

"Were you going to make me fake my own death too?" Jana asked, shocked. That hadn't been mentioned in their initial meeting. Then again, neither had any of this.

"Not at all. But Colin Harlow had a great deal of financial debt. He was a bit of a philanderer, you see, and spent a lot of money on women. His wife found out about this, got proof, and filed for divorce. She was going to take what little he had left."

"Sounds like a charmer," Jacob grumbled. "You guys really pick some nice people."

Bledshaw gave a sad smile. "Whatever his personal failings, he is a great scientist."

"More like a mad scientist," Jana said. "Why did he turn on you?"

"He didn't like our techniques and he wanted to be in charge. And yes, I think your assessment is correct. I do believe he is quite mad."

"Wait," Jana said. "Why would he kill tens of thousands of people just because you're the director and he isn't? And what exactly do you mean by saying he didn't like your techniques?"

"He wanted to go public."

"What's so horrible about that?"

Bledshaw hesitated.

"Come on," Jacob snarled. "Spill."

The two policemen took a step forward, on edge because these three suspicious foreigners were obviously arguing.

Jana forced her tone to become calm and said, “Tell us more about him. I know him only by reputation, and obviously everything I know is wrong.”

“He’s two-faced. We knew that when we recruited him but he was the best in the field and we thought that the nature of the work would make him more inclined to cooperate. We were wrong, and that is entirely our fault. We didn't trust his idea of going public because we thought he'd use that as a way to gain power by stealing the antiquities."

“Surely you could stop him from doing that.”

“Not if he was director. He’d have all the key codes. They can be changed, you see.”

“They weren’t changed here.”

"No, you have to punch in a second code to change the first, and then punch in the new code. Obviously, he didn't share that information with the Indian soldiers. He wanted us to go into that hidden chamber and get killed. He also wanted that chamber discovered. He's unmasking us."

“Why not tell the whole world in an announcement? He’s sure got everyone’s attention.”

“Perhaps he will. Or perhaps he only wants to elite to know and not the general public.”

“Know what exactly?” Jana said. “You don’t kill tens of thousands of people and become the world’s number one most wanted criminal just because you disagree with your boss on policy issues. What’s so important about this collection that you’re hiding? It’s the technology aspect, isn’t it?”

Bledshaw looked uncomfortable. Jacob turned his phone to face him, showing him the river of floating bodies, the shattered buildings, the huddled refugees on the hilltop. Bledshaw grimaced.

“I’m not heartless, you know,” he said defensively. “It’s just that there are larger issues at stake.”

“What’s larger than this?” Jacob growled.

Bradshaw looked him in the eye. "Ancient weapons. Weapons of far greater power and efficacy than the Staff of Ra. If they fell into the wrong hands, if they fell into Harlow's hands, the destruction they could deliver would make these dam attacks seem like nothing in comparison.”

Jana got the impression that he was dodging the question again. "Come on. How is that possible? The Staff of Ra was crude, just a lucky discovery of naturally radioactive material the ancient Egyptians didn't know was fissile. You're telling me someone centuries ago made something more dangerous than that?"

Bledshaw only nodded.

"Mind telling us what?"

He looked down at his feet again. "I … can't. I'm not allowed. Just trust me when I say that if Professor Harlow got access to every dam he wanted, it could very well lead to him becoming dictator of the world."

***

Professor Colin Harlow, who his men knew as Agent Zero, paced back and forth in the narrow confines of his ops center near the Black Sea and for the first time felt unsure of himself. The Curator had not responded to his demands. He knew the man was stubborn, but he didn't think he'd hold firm after two dam explosions and the destruction of two important storage spaces.

Important, but not vital. Neither of them held the key. Neither of them stored irreplaceable information.

The Curator knew that. Maybe that's why he hadn't caved in.

At the bank of computers, his people worked feverishly, monitoring the status of the bombs planted in several of the world's most important dams. The Curator was going to see them blow one by one, watching his precious collection disappear before his eyes.

But not the crown jewels of his collection, and that was a problem.

Hydroelectric dams had been used for the larger, less important assemblages of artifacts, the collections with artifacts that had already been thoroughly studied in the quest to understand the first great civilization of mankind. Now, they sat mostly unaccessed in case further research required another look at the evidence.

But nothing from the original civilization was held in those secret chambers. The really crucial artifacts, and all the original inscriptions from a hundred thousand years ago, were held elsewhere.

Where? He didn't know. That was a closely guarded secret handed down from one Curator to another. As a former assistant director, he hadn't learned even a hint about those locations.

But the Curator would crack. Or his followers would betray him and turn him over.

The second outcome was far more likely. The Curator was too strong-willed to surrender easily. Harlow had to admire him for that. He had a will of iron, a trait Harlow recognized in himself.

Some of the others, however, were made of weaker stuff.

Like Robert Bledshaw.

Harlow had detected a strain of weakness in the man. Sure, he had a brilliant mind and his combat skills were impressive for a man with a background in research, but in meetings he had always wanted to take a moderate course, suggesting freer access to the collections and halting research on the more dangerous aspects of ancient technology. He had even brought up concerns at using artificial intelligence to try and decode the ancient script.

That was the last real hurdle to a full understanding of the ancient civilization, a civilization they didn't even have a name for.

The ancients appeared to have mostly written on perishable materials like paper, or on magnetic tapes similar to the old cassette tapes, the few traces of those now long demagnetized and unreadable. The twenty-three inscriptions they had found on stone and metal were impossible to translate. The script seemed to be syllabic, and their best epigraphers had hypothesized about some of the more common glyphs, but a true translation had always eluded them.

None of the inscriptions included pictures that might hint at their meaning, and there was no bilingual text like the Rosetta Stone with a handy translation into a known language.

Advances in AI, however, promised a breakthrough. It had already radically changed the work of translators of more recent ancient scripts. Bledshaw and a couple of the other weaker ones had pushed for not using the new technology, saying it would "open up a can of worms we might never close again."

The fools! The whole point of hiding and studying the evidence for ancient technology was to reproduce it. So far, they had to work their way back from the primitive imitations of later, lesser cultures. The Staves of Ra and the Parthian batteries. The Antikythera mechanism and the astronomical texts. If they could decipher the ancient script, it would accelerate their research a hundredfold.

He already had the world's most advanced AI program ready to go, thanks to a contact in China who hacked it from an American company. Now, he needed those inscriptions and a few surviving pieces of ancient tech to work from.

"Agent Five, what's been the reaction to the second video of our demands?"

"As expected, sir. Mass panic is setting in. Urban centers downriver from hydroelectric dams are seeing a mass exodus. The governments are trying to keep their people calm and are failing."

Agent Zero nodded. "Good. Chaos will be our ally. Agent Eight, any news on Bledshaw and the others?"

"We haven't heard from any of our people in Patna. It looks like they all got killed or captured. No reports on any American deaths."

"No, I guess that's too much to hope for," Agent Zero murmured. "But perhaps that's a good thing. Yes, perhaps seeing this second attack will be enough to push Bledshaw over the edge and get him to betray the Curator. And that will play right into our hands."

CHAPTER TWENTY

Jana didn't trust Bledshaw, and she didn't believe everything he was saying.

Her suspicion must have been written as plainly on her face as it was on Jacob's, because the director of the Antiquities Division had told her that he wanted to show her some proof of what he said.

Finally! Maybe now they'd get some honesty out of the guy. He brought out his tablet, angled it so the policemen who still watched over them couldn't see, and brought up a video showing a storage room similar to the one they had just seen here in Patna. It was dimly lit by a single emergency bulb, and she couldn't see much.

"This is from two years ago," he said. "It's a dam in Germany. It housed Mesopotamian artifacts. Usually we like to keep the artifacts in the same country they were from, but obviously the situation in Iraq makes that impossible."

A light came on in the storage room, and Jana leaned forward to peer at the image. While it was in black and white and the lighting wasn't the best, she could see racks of cuneiform tablets, some statues, and what looked like an entire assembly of gold jewelry and a crown from a royal burial. Many more artifacts were stored in boxes, their labels too small to read.

A doorway stood on the far wall. She could just make out a narrow staircase in the shadows beyond.

Suddenly, some light illuminated the staircase, the narrow beam of a flashlight. Several men and women filed down the steps. The man in front didn't wear a mask, but all the others did.

"That's Dr. Harlow," the director said, pointing.

Harlow went up to the camera and raised his middle finger. Then he turned and said something to the others, gesturing with impatience.

The half dozen men and woman spread out and started systematically clearing the shelves, forming a human chain to move the artifacts and boxes out of the room and up the stairs to what Jana assumed to be more team members on the upper level.

"How could they do this undetected?"

“They came in the middle of the night posing as contractors. They had obviously bribed someone on the inside to get away with this.”

“They took everything?” In just a minute, a third of the shelves had already been emptied.

“They did.”

“Wait, that flood of Mesopotamian artifacts they hit the illegal antiquities market a couple of years ago, it was from this!”

“That’s right. And that was only a small portion of these artifacts. Most went directly into the hands of private collectors and were never detected by international law authorities.”

Jacob leaned forward. "So, is this how they funded their operations?"

“Yes. They’ve also supplemented their income with other thefts and sales, not from other dams but other museums. Given Harlow’s extensive knowledge and connections, it proved easy for him.”

“Didn’t you change the codes after Harlow defected?”

“Of course, but he’s gained access to them again. We had an assistant director who died in a drowning accident a few months ago. We now believe Harlow bribed or threatened him into giving up the codes, and then Harlow killed him and made it look like an accident.”

“Were there weapons or other dangerous artifacts in this collection?”

“No, thankfully. The key codes to the more sensitive collections are known only to myself. Harlow was an assistant director, so he knew the codes to the less dangerous collections like this one.”

“So he didn’t get any fissile material,” Jana said.

“No.”

“Well, that’s a relief, I guess. What about these so-called ancient superweapons you hinted at? Did he get any of those?”

“No.”

“And what are those weapons?” Jacob asked.

“I can’t discuss that.”

Jacob leaned in close, his face red with anger. “What part of ‘tens of thousands of people are dead’ don’t you understand?”

Bledshaw didn’t bat an eye. Jana had rarely seen anyone who wasn’t intimidated by an angry Jacob Snow, and all of those people had been very, very dangerous.

“Just because you’re the CIA’s top agent doesn’t mean you get access to all our privileged information. I’m just as committed to stopping this madman as you are, in fact more so. I brought you and Dr.

Peters in because Harlow knows our methods and knows our personnel. I need people from the outside who can look at this problem from a different angle and make moves he can't predict."

"I'm up for that," Jacob snapped. "But it would be a hell of a lot easier if you told us more. This video is interesting and all, but it's not telling us anything crucial."

Jana heard a phone ringing. She looked around, thinking it was one of the policemen's, and then realized it was her own.

"Who could be calling me here?" she muttered, pulling it out.

The caller ID said, "Mack's Hardware". A fake business that was the codename for her father.

She stepped away from the arguing men, and the men guarding them, and answered.

"Dad! What's up?"

"Oh, thank God you're all right! I'm in Canada, but I'm heading your way. You in Turkey?"

"India. Patna. We thought the bomb was going to go off here, but it was a decoy. What's going on?"

"I don't like calling on a line that isn't one hundred percent secure but Jacob wasn't picking up on his satellite phone and this can't wait."

She glanced at Jacob and Bledshaw, who were still arguing while the two Indian cops looked on, uncomprehending.

"What did you find out?"

"I talked to an informant, a very reliable one. The best I have. He's the only one who knew anything about the Antiquities Division. Apparently some archaeologist faked his own death to join it, then decided to break with it."

"We just found out the same thing. Looks like your informant knows what he's talking about. What else did he say?"

"He said the fight is over control of a bunch of hidden artifacts that are remnants of an early advanced civilization."

"Which one?"

"One that mainstream science doesn't know about. A hundred thousand years ago, mankind rose to a level of technology higher than what we have now, but a global cataclysm knocked it down. The Antiquities Division is searching the world, finding evidence of this ancient civilization so they can reverse engineer the ancient technology."

"Oh, come on! That's the stuff of cheap TV shows and weirdo Internet sites."

"My informant says they're in earnest. This archaeologist who broke away from the Antiquities Division wants the tech for himself so he can set himself up as a global dictator. That's how he got so many people on his side. One whiff of power will get some lowlifes to follow anyone and do anything."

Jana thought for a moment, looking down at her feet as if she could see through fifty meters of concrete to the unimaginable treasures below. She thought of the accurate star chart, and the analogue computer more advanced than the Antikythera mechanism, one with a calendar going back five thousand years. Then she looked at Robert Bledshaw, who had so much to hide and so many resources at his beck and call.

"Impossible," she whispered, more to reassure herself than to argue with her father.

"Anything's possible. I know it sounds unbelievable, and I know it goes against everything you've come to know. In the end, it doesn't really matter if it's true or not. They believe the technology is there, and they're fighting over it while the rest of the world suffers. Now the question is, what do we do about it?"

"First thing's first. Get over here as quick as you can. Get a private jet from Wallace. After this kind of body count he can't tell you to stay away. We need everyone on this … " Her voice trailed off as she realized she had given the CIA's best field operative, and her own father, an order. She rallied quickly. "Did your informant tell you anything else?"

"No. It's a miracle he knew anything at all. He learned about it the back way when this archaeologist was recruiting people from the underworld. Some of them talked. Not many, but there doesn't have to be more than a whisper in the underworld for it to reach his ears. His intel is solid. Whether what they're saying is true or not, I have no idea, but as I said, they believe in this ancient technology and are willing to destroy entire towns to get it."

"OK, see you soon, Dad."

"Right. I'll call Wallace right now."

Her father hung up. Jana put her phone away and stormed up to Bledshaw and Jacob. Both men stopped their argument and looked at her.

"I just got off the phone with the CIA. You know, that organization you didn't ask to help until it was too late? An agent I know did some digging and found out that some of the people Dr. Harlow recruited blabbed to their friends in the underworld. They said you guys are hiding evidence of advanced technology from an ancient civilization that flourished a hundred thousand years ago, and that you're trying to reverse engineer that tech. They also said that's what Harlow is trying to steal so he can rule the world."

Jana watched the director of the Antiquities Division closely as she said all this. His eyes widened when she mentioned the recruits talking to others, and widen a bit further when she mentioned the advanced ancient civilization from an impossibly early date.

That reaction only lasted for a moment, getting replaced almost instantly by a poker face.

"You informant handed your colleague a bill of goods."

"Maybe, maybe not. While I don't believe all this Von Däniken crap, obviously you guys do. Why else would you go through all this trouble to hunt down and hide artifacts? Why else would Professor Harlow kill so many people and risk his own life? You think you're sitting on the greatest secret in the history of mankind. You guys act like Freemasons on steroids, thinking all your secret wisdom is the key to everything, except the Freemasons don't blow up hydroelectric dams. So what's really going on?"

Bledshaw studied her for a moment, then looked to Jacob before looking back at her.

"Can I rely upon your discretion?"

"You came to us, remember?"

"It's important that this information doesn't become general knowledge."

Jana was losing her patience. He was still dodging the issue after all that had happened? She felt like slapping him. Jacob looked like he was struggling with similar urges.

When Bledshaw stayed silent for a moment, Jana added, "We won't reveal anything unless it saves lives. Right, Jacob?"

"Sure. Your precious little secrets are safe with us."

Bledshaw hesitated, nodded as if coming to a decision, and said,

"Everything your informant said is true. I know as a traditionally trained archaeologist you will not believe me, so I propose to show you. We don't have to go far. There's a site not far from here that will change your perspective. It's one of the reasons we used a dam at this location."

"I can't imagine you could show me anything that would make me believe in a fairy tale like this."

Bradshaw looked her in the eye. "You can't imagine anything like what you are about to see."

CHAPTER TWENTY ONE

While Bledshaw arranged for a helicopter to take them to this mysterious site he thought was so damn important, Jacob got on the satellite phone to Tyler Wallace. It took a minute for him to answer.

"Sorry for the wait, Agent Snow. As you can imagine, I'm insanely busy."

"No problem, boss. What's going on over there?"

"We've arranged with our allies, and even some of our enemies, a coordinated effort to search as many dams as possible."

"Good. I can help with that. Let me explain how this Antiquities Division hides their secret rooms full of treasure."

"I'm sorry, what?"

"Right. I've been going so fast you're several updates behind. Here you go."

Jacob relayed everything he had learned so far, and to hell with Bledshaw's secrecy. He had promised the director of the Antiquities Division not to reveal anything unless it might save lives, and in his opinion keeping Wallace in the loop would save lives.

So he told Wallace everything. He sounded like some breathless conspiracy theorist on YouTube, but he told him everything.

Once he finished, Wallace said, "Thanks for the intel. Not sure how much of it to believe, but thanks anyway."

"I don't know how much to believe myself. How much do you know about the Antiquities Division?"

"I didn't know it even existed until I was told a couple of days ago. They wanted my assessment of how good of a fit you and Jana would be."

"And what did you tell them?"

"That I couldn't think of a better pair of agents for the job."

"Jana isn't an agent."

Wallace laughed. "Tell her that!"

***

Jana wondered what Bledshaw was playing at. They had landed a few miles downstream in the river valley that would have been destroyed if the Patna Dam had blown. They skimmed over a riverside village of about five thousand people before landing on a dirt track between two broad cultivated fields. The edge of the valley, a rocky slope that angled up sharply, stood not far off. She hadn't seen any archaeological sites from the air and she didn't see any now that they had landed.

She hoped Bledshaw wasn't wasting any more of their time. While the terrorists hadn't released another video of demands yet, she had a feeling the clock was ticking. Professor Harlow and his team had already proven their determination.

The director of the Antiquities Division led them away from the helicopter and toward the hills. Jana imagined the dam exploding and a wall of water wiping out everything around them. That village they had just flown over, and the other towns and villages they had passed, would have all been annihilated, along with the city of Patna.

Who are these people who would do such a thing?

Bledshaw knows more about Professor Harlow than he's telling, Jana thought, glowering at his back.

They started to ascend the steep slope. Bledshaw was still in his bloodstained suit, his side bandaged. That didn't slow him down much. He walked a bit stiffly, and chose his footing with care, and yet still moved from boulder to boulder up the slope with impressive speed. Jana and Jacob followed.

Jacob spoke up, sounding impatient. "So where is this archaeological site you're so desperate for us to see?"

"It's not far. See that fissure in the rock? That's it."

Bledshaw pointed out a cleft in the rock about two-thirds of the way up the slope. They headed for it, the hot Indian sun beating down on them and making them sweat.

Once they came to it, Jana saw that the opening to the cave was mostly hidden, thanks to a fold in the rock. At some point in the past, it had been expanded with chisels. A door of thick steel bars had been bolted into the rock surface, blocking the entrance. A red warning sign in Hindi presumably forbade entrance.

"This isn't the original entrance to the cave," Bledshaw told them. "The original entrance is about twenty yards below us and to the left. A survey team from the Bihar Archaeology Directorate discovered it in 1972. Since there is a tradition of cave paintings in this region, the discovery of a new cave sparked their interest. The team tried to clear out the entrance but found it too difficult. Then they searched around for other entrances and found this. Originally, it was too small to squeeze through, so they expanded it. What they found was exceptional."

Bledshaw had brought three flashlights with him from the helicopter and handed them out. Jana was about to ask how they were going to get in when he produced a key, opened the heavy lock, and hauled the door open with a creak. Jana noticed him wince a little at the effort.

He's more injured than he lets on.

They turned on their flashlights and entered a limestone cave, the entrance of which was so narrow that they had to squeeze along sideways for several yards until the passageway opened up enough to allow them to walk comfortably in single file. Jana shivered a little as the air grew cool and her sweaty skin began to suck the heat from her body.

Their flashlights probed the darkness. The passage turned to the left, and they couldn't see further ahead. Jana felt a prickle of anticipation like she always did when exploring some ancient place.

They rounded the corner and came to a chamber about ten feet long and about eight wide. The ceiling was just inches above their heads. Another passage on the far wall continued into darkness.

Jana stopped. High on one wall there she saw faint traces of painting.

She stepped closer, putting her flashlight at an angle to best highlight the faded red and black pigment.

"You have a good eye, Dr. Peters. You'd make a fine addition to our staff."

"Let's neutralize the terrorists first and save the recruiting pitch for later," Jacob said.

Jana ignored them and studied the cave paintings. Two figures, crudely sketched with a few lines but obviously a man and a woman, flanked a strange object that was between and a little above them. She couldn't quite make out what it was supposed to be. It was rectangular and considerably larger than the two figures. An altar?

Then she saw a vague shape on top of the altar. It looked like the top half of a human. An offering? Human sacrifice? Or maybe an idol?

Oddly, the figure appeared to be looking to the right rather than forward like the two flanking figures. She could just make out a head, upper body, and a pair of arms that touched the top of the rectangle.

"I'm not sure what I'm seeing here," Jana admitted.

"How old do you think it is?" Bradshaw asked with a tone that said he already knew the answer.

She moved her flashlight around to different angles and studied the surface more closely.

"Whoa. Hard to tell without measuring, but this scene has to be at least a few thousand years old. Maybe ten thousand."

"How can you tell that?" Jacob asked.

"Limestone caves are always changing. Water drips through fissures in the rock, picking up lime that it then deposits on the ceiling, walls, and floor of the cave. That's how stalactites and stalagmites form. The water will also run down the walls of the cave and leave very thin layers that build up over time."

"Um, OK."

Jana could see she was losing him. He was cute when he pretended an interest. She got to the point.

"See how the images look a bit blurry when I move the light back and forth? That's because limestone has built up over it. It's translucent when it's thin, so we can still see the painting beneath."

"So that means it's old?"

"Yes. It's hard to tell how old without measuring it exactly and gauging the amount of flow over the surface."

"Fine. It's old. But where's the big revelation?"

Jana looked from her lover to Bledshaw. "I'm not exactly sure."

Bledshaw gestured at the cave painting. "What do you think that represents?"

"I'm not sure. I'm not familiar with prehistoric Indian rock art. An altar, perhaps?"

Bledshaw smiled. "Perhaps. Or perhaps you need to see some clearer images in the next chamber."

He moved down the far passageway. Curious, Jana followed. Jacob took up the rear, looking around nervously and fingering the butt of his gun in its holster.

The narrow passage twisted and sloped down. Jana had to brace both hands on opposite walls to keep from slipping. After a few yards, the passage opened up into an irregular chamber five times bigger than the previous one.

Bledshaw focused his beam on a nearby wall and Jana let out a gasp.

It was covered with colorful paintings. She turned and ran her beam along the other walls and found the entire chamber to be almost completely covered in prehistoric art.

She turned and looked at Bledshaw, who gave her a proud smile, then at Jacob, who was staring at all the paintings openmouthed. Even he looked impressed.

"I don't recognize these styles," Jana said. She could pick out two distinct styles that obviously belonged to different artistic periods—the crude geometric figures in red and black that she had seen in the other chamber, and a more elaborate style with realistic figures and a wider palette of colors faded and blurred with time and a thicker layer of limestone.

Which meant the more elaborate style was older.

She frowned and studied several figures more closely. Yes, the more complex style was definitely older. In places, the scenes were almost impossible to make out thanks to a heavy coating of lime. Lime covered the cruder pictures too, but less so and they remained easier to see.

And yet, that didn't make sense. Art almost always progressed from simpler to more complex. There also seemed to be a big gap between the two styles. The older style had a much thicker coating of lime than the newer one.

"This is … odd," she murmured.

"From a traditional perspective, yes," Bradshaw said. "Now focus more on the content."

Jana went over to a cluster of older, more complex images on a relatively flat area of wall. Halfway there, she tripped over an irregularity on the floor and nearly did a faceplant.

Bledshaw chuckled. "Mind your step. I know it's easy to get distracted."

Jana peered at the images, moving the beam of her flashlight back and forth to confirm that they really were coated with a thick, obscuring layer of lime.

"These must be millennia old, perhaps Paleolithic."

"You think?" Bradshaw said in an ironic voice. "Is the content Paleolithic?"

She studied the colorful drawings. They were difficult to make out, especially because the artist or artists had used a lot of yellow which was all but invisible under the yellowish limestone coating.

Even so, the artists had drawn their figures so realistically that she could still puzzle out the scenes.

And those scenes confused her. She saw what looked like a submarine, complete with portholes and people inside, moving along past some fish. She saw a complex pattern that looked for all the world like a circuit board. And she saw a man seated at what looked like a hovercraft, passing over the heads of a man and a woman.

That last image hit her hard, because it was a more elaborate and realistic version of the image she had seen in the other chamber. What she had taken to be false perspective was in fact a depiction of a craft flying overhead, and what she had taken for an altar with a sacrifice or figurine on top was a pilot in a hovercraft or something similar.

Except that wasn't possible. Hovercrafts and circuit boards were twentieth century inventions, not prehistoric ones.

Jana moved over to another section of the wall, one with newer, less detailed drawings. There she found a series of images that didn't make sense unless one thought of them as primitive attempts to draw modern technology—airplanes and rockets, drilling equipment and explosives.

As if in a dream, Jana moved over to another area of the wall, one with some older drawings, a series of circles contained strange shapes that at first she couldn't decipher.

Until she realized they looked like the bacteria and one-celled organisms she had studied under a microscope in high school biology class.

"This isn't possible," she whispered.

"What isn't possible?" Jacob asked, staring at the same images but not seeing what she saw.

"What I'm seeing here." She turned to Bledshaw. "What is this?"

The director of the Antiquities Division gave a little bow.

"It is exactly what it looks like."

"What it looks like isn't possible."

"Why not?"

"What do you mean why not? Because the limestone covering means it's thousands of years old, and none of these things were invented back then!"

"A year ago, you would have said the ancient Egyptians didn't know about radiation. Three hours ago, you would have said there wasn't another example of the Antikythera mechanism. Knowledge progresses, Dr. Peters, and if you allow yourself to really see what you are seeing, your knowledge will progress remarkably."

"This is fake," she said, staring at the wall dubiously.

"Wait, is that a rocket over there?" Jacob asked, pointing.

"It's a picture of what might look like a rocket, which may or may not be old."

Bledshaw chuckled. "Really, Dr. Peters, if it was a simple hunting scene or a drawing of a shaman, you wouldn't be doubting your own eyes."

"But it's not, so I am."

"Fair enough. But this cave had been thoroughly checked by one of our field teams. Dating the layers of limestone formed over the paintings, we have come to a date of seven thousand years for the newer, cruder paintings, which were obviously done by the local Neolithic culture in imitation of the older paintings."

"And the date for the older artwork?" Jana couldn't help but hold her breath while she waited for the answer.

"One hundred and ten thousand years."

CHAPTER TWENTY TWO

Jacob waited for Jana to explode and was not disappointed.

"Impossible! Pure fantasy! You have paintings of microbes and rocket ships here, and you're trying to tell me they date to the Middle Paleolithic?"

“That term doesn’t apply to this particular culture,” Bledshaw said.

“Come on. This is nonsense! There’s no evidence for a technological civilization from that period.”

“You’re looking at it.”

Jacob looked around at the faint drawings, blurred by millennia of limestone deposits. While he wasn’t an expert, they sure looked old. But Jana had a point. You needed a lot more than a few drawings in a cave in India to turn all of human history upside down.

Jana stomped around the cave, waving her hand dismissively. “These could be modern. Perhaps the flow of lime-impregnated water is stronger than you think. There are examples of mining tools from the Gold Rush getting encased in limestone. The nutcases like to use those as evidence for ancient advanced civilizations.”

“I assure you we are not nutcases, and this cave was measured with great care. There isn’t much of a flow of water, as you yourself can see.”

“If this is so groundbreaking, why wasn’t it ever published in a journal or something?” Jacob asked.

"Because we hid it. We recruited the local archaeologist who found this cave, and in return for a significant increase in income and the chance for some important research, he kept his mouth shut."

“Why would you cover up something like this?” Jacob asked.

“Because it’s not unique. One such site could be dismissed. But there are many sites that point to a global civilization at a time when most of humanity was living in caves and using stone tools. We hide all of them.”

“So you’re saying the high-tech civilization lived side by side with the cavemen?” Jacob asked while Jana gave a derisive snort. “That doesn’t make any sense.”

"Doesn't it? Just a hundred years ago, many parts of the world were living in the Stone Age while others enjoyed airplanes and electricity."

“So where’s the evidence?” Jana asked.

“At several hidden archaeological sites such as this one, and stored in a number of hydroelectric dams around the world.”

“And you’ve managed to keep all that a secret all this time? Come on.”

"Some information has slipped through, Dr. Peters. You and your colleagues have dismissed this evidence as made up or misinterpreted. You've seen some yourself, perhaps brought to your attention by some overeager undergraduate student who read an alternative book or saw a video on YouTube. You dismissed it out of hand. Even if you had tracked down the source, most of those publications get it all wrong. Those hack writers say it was an ancient race of magicians or enlightened masters or aliens. They were nothing of the sort. They were as human as you or I, and they were far from enlightened. In fact, they destroyed themselves out of hubris."

“Like Atlantis?” Jacob asked.

“That continent never existed. It’s a simple fable, but that fable contains echoes of the real ancient civilization that did destroy itself.”

For a moment, no one spoke. Jacob shone his light around the cave, both at the faded old drawings that realistically showed so many impossible things, and at the more recent, cruder drawings that had been done in imitation, or perhaps worship. Could it really be true?

At last, Jana spoke up. “So you’re saying this ancient culture was so powerful they wiped themselves out and nearly all trace of themselves?”

She didn’t sound convinced, and yet now she didn’t sound completely dismissive either.

“They tended to live in the more temperate areas to the north in places like North America, northern Europe, and Russia, although they did have some settlements in the equatorial regions such as India. After they wiped themselves out and the outlying settlements collapsed or got run over by more primitive peoples, the Ice Age scraped the evidence of their civilization from the surface of the Earth.”

“What about nonperishable modern materials? Why don’t we find plastic or steel?”

"We do find some artifacts of steel, artifacts mainstream archaeology dismisses. As for plastics, they don't seem to have used it, or used some variant that was biodegradable. Our own society has developed biodegradable plastics, but they haven't been put into widespread use because they're more expensive."

"I'm going to need to see a lot more evidence before I believe any of this."

"Join the Antiquities Division and you will see all the evidence you could possibly desire."

Jana stared at him, and Jacob suddenly felt worried. What if she did join? It must be tempting as hell for her. And where would that leave him? She might go away, and they wouldn't live together anymore.

Jana opened her mouth to speak, and Jacob cut in.

"First thing's first. We need to stop Dr. Harlow and his goons from blowing up any more dams. Let's get back to the chopper and get back to work."

Bledshaw headed for the passageway that would lead them out. Jana pulled out her phone and held it up toward the wall.

"No."

The single word from Bledshaw's mouth was so forceful, so blunt, that Jana let her hand fall.

Bradshaw walked over to her. Jacob's hand moved toward his gun.

"May I see your phone?" Bledshaw asked, extending his hand.

Jana showed him her gallery. She hadn't taken a photo.

"Thank you. Let's go."

Jacob let his hand drop. In all his years as an operative, he had learned to gauge people, and he was rarely ever wrong. What he had figured out about Bledshaw was that he would have not let them leave with photos of the cave paintings, no matter what it took.

He remembered Bledshaw's intelligence, his resources, the strength he had shown when he had pulled both Jacob and Jana away from the crumbling cliff, his shrugging off of a bullet wound, and Jacob told himself that he should be very careful never to underestimate him.

Jacob also realized that while they were nominally allies at the moment, that may change, and then he'd have to take care.

Because Robert Bledshaw would make a very dangerous enemy.

***

When they got back to the chopper, the pilot was standing in its shade, smoking a cigarette while about twenty barefoot children from the nearest village stared at the machine. The boys wore shorts and faded t-shirts. The girls wore colorful saris and headscarves.

"You look like you've made some little friends," Bradshaw said with a smile.

"I'm just glad they didn't get all killed," the pilot said, dropping his cigarette and crushing it underfoot. "Both of the satellite phones rang while you were gone."

Jacob and Bledshaw climbed into the helicopter and grabbed their satellite phones, then walked to opposite ends of the field to talk privately.

Or almost privately. Half the children went with Bledshaw, the other half with Jacob. While a chopper landing next to the village was an interesting diversion, they had probably never seen a satellite phone before.

Jacob squatted on his haunches Asian style, and the kids squatted in a circle around them.

"Any of you a security hazard?" Jacob asked.

All he got was blank looks and giggles.

"I guess I'll just have to take a chance. None of you look like you're packing, anyway. Maybe I'll get lucky, and you speak some obscure Indian dialect that happens to be the same language Bledshaw's using for his comms. Then your buddies can tell me everything he said."

That got more blank looks and giggles.

He called Wallace, who picked up immediately.

"Agent Snow, tell me the situation."

"We're working with the Antiquities Division to try and figure out where the terrorists will make their next move. Bledshaw is being a bit more cooperative, but only a bit."

A slim hand reached for one of the dials. Jacob grasped it and gently moved it away to a chorus of giggles.

"What was that?" Wallace asked.

"Nothing, sir. What's going on at your end?"

"We've cast a wide net for the suspect from the Harper Dam, Fred Garrick. As far as we can determine, he never left the dam area. He might have been incapacitated by the terrorists and left to die in the explosion so he could never talk."

"That's inconvenient, but you're not going to find me shedding a tear for that ass wipe. Oh, we did get a prisoner. One of the turncoat Indian soldiers. Hopefully we can get him to tell us something useful."

"Good. We've forwarded the information you sent about the Patna dam to all the nations participating in our global sweep. At the moment, 85 countries are checking their dams based on this information. That's more than five hundred dams, and we expect more nations to join soon."

"Great. I get the feeling that they planned all of this out ahead of time, and they're waiting to blow the next one. With the added security, no way are they going to be able to plant any new bombs."

“That’s our thinking too, Agent Snow. We’ll keep you updated as regularly as we can. What’s your next move?”

Jacob paused. “I’m … not exactly sure. We’re still pumping Bledshaw for information. You know he claims the Antiquities Division is hiding evidence of an advanced ancient civilization from a hundred thousand years ago? Says they have super weapons and this Professor Harlow guy wants to get his hands on them.”

“That’s odd. What does Jana think of that?”

“She’s unconvinced. But what really matters is Bledshaw and Harlow think it’s true.”

“I see. Did Bledshaw authorize you to reveal this information?”

“I told him I’d only reveal his precious little secrets if I thought it would save lives. I think any intel might save lives, so screw Bledshaw.”

“Sounds like you don’t like him.”

"I don't trust him any further than I can throw him and you know what? Despite his country club routine, I might not be able to throw him all that far."

“Sounds like you admire the man.”

“He does play the game well.”

“All right, Agent Snow. Keep me posted. I need to go. The president is breathing down the CIA director’s neck. We got to get cracking.”

“Talk to you soon.”

He hung up.

One of the boys sitting close to him pointed to the satellite phone and asked, “Telephone?”

“Yes.”

The kid pointed to him. “Army?”

“No.”

Not a lie but not exactly the truth. Jeez, do I even have to be on the defensive with a ten-year-old?

I want to go back to the cabin and finish that chair.

He tousled the boy's hair, stowed the satellite phone, and started walking back to the chopper. One of the girls took his hand, setting off a chorus of giggles.

Jana's grin was clearly visible twenty yards away.

Hmm. Now she's going to think I'm good with children. Women always get ideas when they think you're good with children.

Jacob found that thought wasn't as terrifying as he would have a few years ago. Maybe that was because they had a good chance of all dying on this mission. That would stop any nefarious plans Jana might have for his personal freedom.

The girl kept holding his hand until they reached Jana, then skipped over to her and started chattering away in Hindi. The rest of the kids began to examine the helicopter again as the pilot looked on, amused.

Bledshaw approached. "Sorry to break up your familial moment, but we've just received another communique from the terrorists."

Bledshaw took out his phone, hit a link, and held it at an angle so the children couldn't see.

It was a crudely made mashup of Turkish media images of the dam's destruction, obviously made in haste since the attack had occurred barely an hour ago. A computer voiceover intoned,

"You have ignored our demands. We want the Curator. You have not brought him to the specified location. You have not even identified him. That is because he lives in secret and hasn't come forth. Despite the death toll, he hasn't revealed his identity. He would rather let innocent people die than give himself up."

The video showed a closeup of bodies bobbing in swirling water.

"We will not tell you who the Curator is. He must identify himself. He must stop the killing by giving himself up. But we doubt he will. He is too selfish. The Curator would rather let thousands of innocent people die than give up his privileged position. Well, we will give him his wish. Twenty-four hours from now, another bomb will go off and another dam will burst. The death toll for the third dam will be far, far greater than what you have seen so far. The Curator's continued silence will be proof to the world how heartless he is.

"You have twenty-four hours. Then you will see who the real terrorist is."

The kids were hopping up and down, trying to see what was on the phone. Bledshaw held it a bit higher and replayed the video.

As the heartless computer voice gave its demands and bodies floated across the screen, Bledshaw slumped against the helicopter, his face a mask of misery.

He switched the phone off and turned to the helicopter pilot.

"Could you give us a moment, please?"

The pilot shrugged and walked away. The kids stayed put, one little boy of about eight tugging on Bledshaw's sleeve, pointing at the phone.

Bledshaw got on YouTube, found a cartoon, and handed him the phone. The village kids squealed with joy and gathered around to watch.

Then the director of the Antiquities Division straightened up, looked them in the eye and said,

"I can't do this anymore. Allow me … allow me to tell you who the Curator is."

CHAPTER TWENTY THREE

Jana held her breath. Finally, some honesty from Robert Bledshaw.

The director of the Antiquities Division looked at Jana and Jacob and said,

"The Curator is my boss."

"What!?" Jacob snapped. "Seriously? You've been holding out on that this whole time? You told us plan and simple there was no such person."

"So that's who you kept having to get permission from," Jana said. "You acted like you were in charge but you kept having to await orders."

Bledshaw nodded.

"After the attack in Nevada when Professor Harlow made his demands, I contacted the Curator and urged him to give himself up. He said he would. Then the clock ticked down, and he never revealed himself. I called him again just now and he refuses point blank. He says that Harlow wants to torture him into revealing all the codes, all the secrets. He probably would. If Harlow gains access to our collected knowledge, it would prove disastrous. Harlow could set himself up as world emperor."

Jana rolled her eyes. "Come on. Are you trying to tell me this so-called super civilization had that much power?"

"Their knowledge nearly wiped out humanity once. It could do so again."

"You're crazy," she said, shaking her head. "You're all completely crazy."

"You haven't seen the things I've seen."

"I've seen plenty," Jacob growled. "And what I'm seeing is your damn boss letting people die."

Bradshaw looked at his feet. "I thought he'd be a better man than that."

"We need to convince him to give himself up," Jana said.

"He never will. I see that now. He's as driven as Harlow, and as hard hearted. You should have seen their power struggle when Harlow was still in the Antiquities Division. So bitter. So factional. It split the division right down the middle. Many top-ranking members left with Harlow. They saw the chance for power, and that's very seductive."

“Where did Harlow get all of these lackeys?” Jana asked. “Those Indian soldiers sure didn’t come from the Antiquities Division.”

"A combination of greed and hunger for power. Harlow can be very persuasive, plus he has a lot of money to wave under people's noses. He tried to recruit me, but I saw through him. My error was not seeing through the Curator."

“What’s the Curator’s name?” Jana asked.

Bradshaw shook his head. "I don't know."

“Come on.”

“I swear I don’t know. I don’t even know where he is. He always maintains the greatest secrecy. We keep a number of safehouses. He could be at any of them. Or at one I’m not aware of. That’s more likely given the situation.”

“We need to find him! We need to convince him to give himself up.”

“To be tortured? To give up the secrets he’s sworn to protect? He’ll never agree to that.”

“Then we need to find Harlow.”

Bledshaw gave a helpless shrug. “I have no idea where he is. None of us do. That’s why we reached out to you.”

“Can we speak to your boss?”

Bledshaw paled. “He’d kill me if he knew I told you of his existence.”

“Kill you?”

“Yes. Kill me. I took an oath. I broke that oath because the Curator let the Turkish dam blow. I owe him nothing anymore, but I don’t want to die.”

“Don’t worry,” Jacob said. “As you know, I spoke with a colleague who found out a bunch about your organization. Not as much as you’ve told us, but I’ll say that my colleague’s informant told me that you’re only second in command with the Curator at the top.”

Bradshaw considered that for a moment. "He might believe such a story. Indeed, he worried that bringing you in would make the CIA do some research and find out more about the Antiquities Division than it already knew. Yes, it's worth the risk. I'll ask if I can patch him through to you. It's going to take some convincing, though."

“More convincing in that strange language you all use?” Jana asked.

Bledshaw gave a sad smile. "Manx. We're secretive even when talking with each other."

The director grabbed his satellite phone and walked away. The village kids stayed put, hypnotized by the cartoon on his cell phone.

"What's Manx?" Jacob asked.

"A branch of Gaelic used in the Isle of Man. It all but died out in the twentieth century although there's been a bit of a revival. There are no native speakers anymore but I guess there are still courses you can take. Not a bad language to use as a code. The chances of bumping into a stranger who speaks it are nearly zero."

Jacob looked at Bledshaw as he crouched in the middle of the field, talking on the satellite phone.

"Huh. This guy's pretty damn smart. Looks like he's beginning to have a conscience too."

They could see him arguing and waving his hands in the air. Words in Manx carried over the field to them. A couple of the village kids glanced curiously over their shoulders before getting sucked back into the cartoon.

Bradshaw knows how to deal with kids. I wonder if he has any of his own.

Jana glanced at the helicopter pilot, who was also with the Antiquities Division. He stood at the far end of the field, smoking another cigarette while staring at his director with an intense expression.

I hope we don't have any trouble with him.

After a couple of minutes, Bradshaw stood and signaled for them to come over. The pilot began to move toward him too but Bledshaw waved him off.

Jacob and Jana crossed the field and joined them.

"He's agreed to speak with you." The way Bledshaw said that did not fill Jana with optimism.

They crouched in front of the satellite phone, its speaker looking at them like a single dark eye.

"Hello, Mr. Curator, this is Dr. Jana Peters speaking. Agent Jacob Snow is with me."

"What do you want to speak with me about?" The voice sounded upper class, American, and irritated.

"One of our CIA informants told us of your existence, Mr. Curator, and we wanted to speak with you directly in order for us to find a solution to this problem together."

"The solution is for you to find Dr. Harlow and kill him," the Curator snarled. "That's what I hired you for."

You think we're assassins?

Jana and Jacob exchanged a glance. Bledshaw stood a little apart, looking ill at ease.

Jacob cut in. "Jacob Snow here. We'll do whatever it takes, Mr. Curator, but I don't think we have the time to track him down before the next deadline. Perhaps you could give yourself up and we could arrange an ambush."

"Don't be ridiculous. You think he won't see through that? Harlow is more intelligent than all of you put together."

Jacob glared at the satellite phone but managed to keep his voice level. "That may very well be so, but I've taken down people who are smarter than me before. And I think the best way to do that is to ambush him while delivering you. Don't worry, we'll—"

"I'm not worried because we'll do nothing of the sort."

"Tens of thousands of people have died!" Jana snapped. "How can you just sit by and let that happen again?"

"They didn't die because of me. They died at the hands of a terrorist. And if I give in to his demands, he'll end up far more powerful than you can imagine. No, I will not give myself up to that madman and that's final."

I think we're dealing with two madmen here.

"Mr. Curator," Jana, trying not to communicate what she felt about him through her tone. "I'm struggling to understand the role of ancient technology in all this. Mr. Bledshaw has not been forthcoming about information. He—"

"He better not have been!"

"No, he hasn't. But circumstances have forced him to reveal that there's some sort of ancient technology like the Staff of Ra that Dr. Harlow is after. That makes sense. He wouldn't go through all this trouble and you wouldn't be so secretive if something you're hiding couldn't be weaponized."

"True enough," the Curator grumbled.

"Could you tell me more about this in order to help our investigation?" Jana asked. She glanced at Harlow. "Maybe which ancient civilization invented it? Was it the Egyptians?"

Bradshaw gave a nod of approval for letting him off the hook.

"It doesn't matter who it was. The main thing is to catch Harlow."

“I understand that. Could you give us an idea where he might strike next?”

“If I knew that’s I’d tell you, obviously. Now get back to work and find out where … wait, what’s that? What’s going on?”

The Curator sounded like he was speaking to someone else. The mic cut off. The three of them looked at each other, confused.

A moment later, the mic switched back on.

“I need to speak to Bledshaw. Alone!”

Jana and Jacob meekly walked away. They didn’t get far before they heard Bledshaw getting a royal chewing out in Manx.

“What’s he griping at him for?” Jacob asked.

"Who knows? The guy sounds just as power-hungry as Dr. Harlow."

As they watched while Bradshaw stood and took a torrent of abuse, Jana couldn't help but feel a little sorry for him. Perhaps he was a decent man fighting the good fight in a bad organization. She had certainly met plenty of them in her time. Her father had met a whole lot more.

After a minute, she was surprised to see Bledshaw gesture for the helicopter pilot to come over. Once he did, Bledshaw returned to the helicopter while the pilot crouched down and listened. They could no longer catch any words. The Curator had lowered his voice.

Uh-oh.

“What happened?” Jana asked as Bledshaw rejoined them.

“The engineers in a dam in Mexico just found a secret chamber. The Antiquities Division monitors all the secret chambers via remote security cameras. The Mexicans didn’t know the code, of course, but once they knew to look for an entrance they found it and opened it with drills.”

He gave Jacob a significant look.

“Sorry,” Jacob said.

“Don’t be. It was necessary. There wasn’t a bomb there but it was necessary.”

“Well, sorry you got in trouble.”

“Are you in danger?” Jana asked.

“I don’t think so. Even the Curator can see why I opened the chamber here in Patna. He’s just blowing off steam. Showing who’s in charge. He likes doing that.”

“And what’s he talking to the pilot about?”

Bledshaw glanced over at the chopper pilot and his face turned grim.

"I don't know."

CHAPTER TWENTY FOUR

Jacob tried to read the helicopter pilot's expression as he spoke quietly to the Curator. From his position Jacob couldn't hear a word, only the musical laughter of the children still being entertained by a cartoon on Bledshaw's smart phone.

He could see the guy's expression, though, and he did not look happy. He nodded in agreement at something his boss told him, a resolved look settling on his face.

The chopper pilot stood, turned off the satellite phone—Jacob found it interesting that he knew how to use it, since most people had never even seen one—and carried it back to them.

Just then the kids stood up. The cartoon was over and they held up the phone to Bledshaw and chattered away, obviously asking for more.

He smiled and took it. "I'm afraid the party's over for all of us."

He pocketed the phone to the kids' moans of disappointment.

The helicopter pilot came up to them. "Time to get back to the airport. We don't know where we're going next, but it's better to be at the jet ready to go."

He said this to Jacob. He didn't even look at the director of the Antiquities Division.

Bledshaw grimaced and climbed aboard.

Jacob and Jana herded the kids away from the chopper and the pilot started the engine.

As they ascended the kids waved. Bledshaw waved back, looking like he'd rather be anywhere than inside this chopper.

As they headed back toward Patna airport, Jacob got a call from the Patna police. They had exchanged numbers and the cops had promised to get in touch if they had any new leads.

"Agent Snow here. Did you find out anything?"

"Captain Tripathi here. We cleared out the false bomb in the dam. There was never any danger. It is sad that it caused such bloodshed. There has been bloodshed in town too. At least we were spared what has happened in Turkey."

"Did you question the prisoner?"

"We used the most forceful techniques his condition would allow." Jacob did not let his imagination fill in the details. "He says he was recruited for a sizeable amount of money and the promise of a passport to a European Union nation. We checked his house and found 20,000 in euros and a book giving Indian citizens advice on relocating to Germany."

"Who recruited him?"

"His own sergeant, who died in the fight."

"And who recruited the sergeant?"

"The private claims he does not know. We are pressuring him on this point but he insists he was kept in ignorance. He says he was told the bomb was fake and so felt no danger, and was also told that most of the regiment had been recruited, but that he must keep quiet because a few of his comrades-in-arms remained loyal."

"So they told him to keep quiet not only to keep the attack a secret but also so he wouldn't discover he was on a suicide mission."

"He is regretting his decision now."

"I bet he is. Sounds like he doesn't know much, though."

"No. I believe his ignorance is actual and not feigned. We will keep pressuring him."

"Try not to pressure him so much he misses his execution date."

"We will resist the temptation."

"All right, call me if you get any more information."

Another dead end. And we haven't heard from the Slovenes either. Guess they haven't tracked down the arms smugglers. Damn it!

Jacob's satellite phone rang. He picked up. Tyler Wallace's voice came over the line.

"Bad news, Agent Snow."

"You don't have to say that. You only call when you have bad news."

"Sorry."

"Not as sorry as I'm about to be. What's up?"

"Using your instructions we've found a whole host of bombs in dams around the world. Brazil, the Czech Republic, Germany, Guatemala, Sri Lanka, the U.S., Canada … the list goes on and on. All are in hidden chambers filled with archaeological artifacts. All are timed to blow and wired in such a way as to make it hard to defuse safely."

"Oh, crap. How many dams so far?"

"Seventeen in as many nations."

Jacob had the sudden urge to wet his pants.

"And there's something worse," Wallace said.

"Worse? What could be worse?"

"Many are timed to blow before the next deadline."

"What? Why would they do that?"

"No idea. Maybe they're decoys. Maybe they've decided to maximize the body count."

"Wait. They set all of this up beforehand, so they had the timers set beforehand. And they probably weren't banking on being able to get back inside. Too much of a risk. Hell, it's a miracle they were able to get it all set up in the first place. So were they planning on blowing them all anyway?"

"I don't know, but we and our allies are scrambling the best bomb disposal experts in the business to the affected dams. We don't have time to get to some of them, so rather than use personnel who are less than top-notch, we're having some of our top people give instructions via satellite video link to people on the ground."

"Good. Any in India we can help with?"

"No more in India yet. The search is still going on. We presume the Russians and Chinese are checking their own dams. We warned them, at least. Oh, we had to stop Aaron Peters from flying to you. He's helping with a dam stateside."

"OK. Keep me posted."

"They might all be decoys except one or two. Unfortunately they're wired in such a way that we can't shift the detonators to check, so we have to go on the assumption that they're all live."

"Great. I'll have Jana try to think of which would be the next logical target."

"Thank you, Agent Snow. I'll be in touch."

They were just landing in Patna airport as Tyler Wallace hung up. Once the rotor blades stopped and they could hear each other without using the open comm on their headphones, Jacob got in a huddle with Bledshaw and Jana.

"Just got a call from Tyler Wallace, he says … "

Jacob's voice trailed off as the chopper pilot climbed into the back to join them.

"Could you leave us for a couple of minutes, Mark?" Bledshaw said.

"No."

The pilot and the director stared at each other for a long moment.

“I could make you go,” Bledshaw said in a quiet voice.

The pilot looked him up and down. “Yeah. Probably.”

“But he’d hear about it.”

“Yep.”

The pilot turned to Jacob. “You were saying?”

Jacob looked at Bledshaw, who gave an irritated nod, and so Jacob relayed everything Wallace had told them.

When he finished, Bledshaw said, “I think Harlow foresaw that we would alert the nations of the world of the secret chambers. This is part of his plan to expose the Antiquities Division.”

“How many of those bombs do you think are real?”

“I have no idea.”

Jana leaned forward. “Wallace is right. We need to figure out which is the most likely one to blow next. Harlow has been targeting ancient technology. First the Parthian collection, and then the Byzantine. I’m going to need to see your entire database in order to look for connections. Maybe I can narrow it down.”

“I’d be happy to help. I’ll give you full access to the database.” Bledshaw shot a challenging look at the pilot. “Do you have any objections?”

“My orders to are observe,” the pilot said, “and report.”

“Very well,” Bledshaw grumbled. He pulled out a laptop, kept it turned away from the rest of them, and typed in a password. Then he typed in a second one. Then a third.

Jesus, these people are paranoid. Could they really be on to something here? Could all this stuff about an ancient wonder weapon really be true?

Bledshaw turned the laptop to face Jana.

“Here’s the entire database, at least all of the database I’m privy to. You might want to look through the Byzantine collection first.”

“Sure,” Jana sighed. “Let’s see what irreplaceable treasures they destroyed.”

Jacob and Bledshaw looked over her shoulder as she worked. The pilot sat opposite, watching their every move.

***

Jana had grown accustomed to working under pressure, but this was too much damn pressure. The clock was literally ticking, she had three guys staring at her, and she had no clear idea what she was looking for.

Plus looking through an unparalleled collection of ancient and medieval artifacts was pretty distracting in its own right.

The Byzantine collection had contained true wonders. Not only did it include fragments of the gold mosaics and richly painted Christian icons the civilization was justly famous for, there were also several steam-driven mechanisms. Most were curios like a golden horse that trotted along while blowing steam from its nostrils. Others were of uncertain use. One was a steam-powered cannon dating to the later fourteenth century, although it didn't look as powerful as the black powder artillery that was already becoming common in the armies of the time.

She saw nothing that would link these or any of the other objects to other collections.

"I don't get it! There's no real pattern and these aren't your best objects anyway. You said the best ones are hidden away."

"They are."

"Have you seen them?"

"Some of them. They do, indeed, exist."

Jana glanced at her watch. She had done that several times in the past hour and need to stop it. Focusing on how little time you had was the worst thing you could do when you had limited time.

"What's the Curator's specialty?"

"He's a Byzantinist, so he felt the destruction of the Turkish dam as a personal insult."

"He obviously didn't shed a tear over the 50,000 Turks who got killed. Are there any other Byzantine collections?"

"No. And he has no other favorite collections."

Jana bit her lip. She scanned the descriptions of the many Byzantine manuscripts in the collection. The Parthian inscriptions had given her a clue that led to the Mauryan collection. Except that had been a trap. Damn it!

Calm down. Calm down and focus.

As she scanned the descriptions of the manuscripts—biographies of Byzantine emperors, a geography of the eastern Mediterranean, hagiographies, she came across a couple of lines that jumped out at her.

It was a military manual from the 11th century. The line read, "text references dropping Greek fire from flying machine. Attempt to reconstruct flying machine found near Bosphorus during construction of aqueduct. Experiment a failure but reference too vague to determine more details."

She pointed this out to Bledshaw. “What’s this? They found an ancient flying machine?”

Jana could hardly believe those words had passed her lips not dripping with sarcasm.

"Ah, I remember this entry. Yes, the military manual makes an oblique reference to finding the remains of an ancient flying machine. Its purpose was obvious to the Byzantines, but they weren't able to reproduce it. The military manual theorized how useful it would have been to drop Greek fire on their enemies."

“It sure would have been.” Greek fire was an early form of napalm squirted out of hoses against enemy ships. It had helped the Byzantine Empire dominate the eastern Mediterranean.

An idea sparked in her head, ignited by a vague memory. She returned to the Parthian database and took a minute to find the right entry.

One of the inscribed tablets included a line referencing, “the wise ancestors who flew in the air and swam in the sea like fishes.”

She blinked, then went to the Mauryan database.

“I see what you’re doing!” Bledshaw cried. “Scroll down to the third temple inscription.”

Jana did so and found an inscription relating to various Hindu deities and a line saying, “our forefathers blessed by the gods with godlike powers. In the grand temple in Pataliputra lies the remains of one of the blessed flying chariots. Constant prayer for three generations has yet to make it take flight. Future generations—be vigilant in prayer and the gods and goddesses will grant us such blessings once again!”

“Whoa,” Jacob said.

Jana turned to the director of the Antiquities Division. “Are there any more references to this ancient culture? Are they common?”

“No, they are not common. I can think of only two more. One in Nepal and another in Brazil.”

As Jana brought up those databases, she said, “What if he’s targeting collections that contain references to ancient technology? He wants to wipe those out.”

“That would make sense. Without access to the collections containing the ancient remains, he’s undercutting our research as much as he can by getting rid of all later references to it.”

The Brazilian collection contained rock art similar to what Jana had seen in the Indian cave. The Nepalese collection had inscriptions from one of the medieval city-states that flourished there centuries before, recounting ancient artifacts kept in the Hindu temples.

"Are you sure these are the only ones?" Jana asked.

"Quite sure. I should have seen the pattern myself. You have a remarkable mind, Dr. Peters."

Jana turned to Jacob and found him already on his satellite phone.

He spoke briefly with Tyler Wallace and then turned to them.

"Brazil's dam is scheduled to blow in an hour. The dam in Nepal is scheduled to blow in a little less than two hours."

"I can get us to Nepal," the pilot said. "Kathmandu is only 300 kilometers away. I can get us there in an hour. We can take a helicopter from there."

"Great. We'll take that one. Wallace is having your father deal with the one in Brazil via a video feed."

"He's only got an hour. Will that be enough?"

Jacob looked grim. "It better be. There's a city of one million people just downstream."

CHAPTER TWENTY FIVE

Carlos Pereira, the chief electrical engineer for the Maranhão Provincial Hydroelectric Dam in northeastern Brazil, could feel the sweat dripping off of him. He kept wiping his hands on his trousers to keep them dry so he could work. The rest of his body was absolutely soaked.

He faced a mass of wires that looked more like a plate of spaghetti than an electrical connection, and he knew that was deliberate. Some of these wires would blow the explosives arrayed along the floor at his feet. Many more would do nothing.

Only one defused the bomb.

They had found this room underneath what they thought was the lowest level of the dam, following instructions from a CIA communique. It was filled with ancient inscriptions and textiles, like a hidden museum.

He didn't have time to wonder at that. He had something far more important to command his attention.

Slowly and carefully, he pried the multicolored wires apart to see where they led. His colleagues scrambled to set up radio relays so the signal from the American satellite could reach the bowels of the huge concrete hydroelectric dam. The CIA had told them they had an explosives expert on the line who would walk him through defusing the bomb step by step.

The timer said fifteen minutes. Carlos Pereira didn't have time to wait. He got busy cutting obvious false connections in order to clear the view so that the American could work more easily.

He only cut the wires he felt absolutely sure connected nothing. Even so, every snip of his wire cutters made him wince in terror.

While he worked and some of his colleagues set up the relay, the other engineers stood behind him. Bernardo, the chief engineer and his boss, resisted his usual arrogant know-it-all attitude and kept his mouth shut. Miguel paced back and forth. Augusto had thrown up in the corner.

"You still have time to leave," Carlos said as he tossed aside another dud wire.

“We’re here for you, Carlos,” Bernardo said.

He had never liked his boss, but the man was showing a new aspect of his nature today. Miguel and Augusto were good friends and wouldn’t leave his side, although Carolos wanted them to.

Because he wasn’t at all sure he could defuse this bomb, and he knew nothing about this CIA man. He’d feel a lot better if his friends had a chance to escape.

Not that he would have left if one of them was stuck in this terrible situation.

He tried not to think of his friends. He tried not to think of his beautiful wife Daiane or his two cute little twin daughters, Iara and Camila, just five years old. They all lived in the city of São Luís downriver.

If he did this right, he and Daiane would grow old together, watching their girls grow up. All the other one million people in São Luís would also survive.

If he failed, they would all die.

He tried not to think of that as he snipped another wire.

“Good job, Carlos,” Augusto said. His breath smelled of vomit, not that Carlos could blame him. He wanted to vomit too. He wanted to curl up in the corner and wail like a baby.

He could do none of those things. He had to keep searching, keep cutting.

Another wire, and another. It seemed no clearer. There seemed no end to these wires!

He sent up a prayer to the Virgin Mary and cut another wire.

The timer said ten minutes.

Ten minutes? Where had the last five minutes gone?

"The relay is set up," Bernardo said in a quiet voice, desperately trying to sound calm. He placed something on his head. "This is a GoPro camera so the American can see. Here's a mic." He adjusted something beside his cheek.

A voice came over the line, speaking English. Carlos had gotten top marks in university in English. While he regularly read engineering manuals in English, he hardly ever used it in conversation. He hoped it wouldn’t fail him.

“Hello. This is Aaron Peters with the CIA. Your boss told me you’re Chief Engineer Carlos Pereira. How are you doing today?”

At first, Carlos thought he had misunderstood the man's English. Then he realized Aaron was trying to put him at ease.

"I've had better days. Can you see what I'm doing?"

"Yes. Could you look at the timer?"

Eight minutes. Santa Maria, why was time going so fast?

"All right. I see you've stripped some of the dud wires. That's good. You're going great."

The man's voice was so calm. How could he be so calm?

Because he's not the one who's going to get blown up, that's why.

"OK, Carlos. Let's take a look. Move the wires around a bit. That's good. That green one you have your middle finger on, let's take a look at that. OK, that's a trap. Do you have any way to mark it?"

"A Sharpie!" Carlos called out. "Someone give me a Sharpie."

All three men in the room reached over his shoulders with Sharpies. He took one.

"These are your friends?"

"Yes."

Bernardo counted as a friend now. He hadn't fled. That forgave all his bad behavior.

"Good to see they got your back."

Carlos marked the suspect wire with the Sharpie.

"OK, Carlos, let's get back to work. No, don't look at the timer. Focus on the wires."

"I-I think this is a dud."

"Yes, that's a dud. Very good."

Carlos cut it.

"Oh, excellent. See how that clears up the view?"

Carlos didn't see, but he took the CIA agent's word for it.

"Now move those wires on the righthand side … "

Carefully, methodically, and way too slowly, they worked through the wires, snipping duds, marking traps with the Sharpie, and locating possible wires that could defuse the bomb.

They had five candidates for the one wire they sought, and a bunch more wires they didn't know about.

We don't have the time.

"No, don't look at the timer."

Two minutes!

"We're almost there, Carlos."

"We only have two minutes."

A hand rested on his shoulder.

"You can do it, Carlos," Miguel said.

Carlos Pereira took a deep breath and got back to work.

“This is a trap,” he said, marking it with the Sharpie.

"Yes, it is. Good job. Pull those middle three wires apart. OK, cut the middle one. Mark the right one.”

“And the left one?”

“Not sure yet. We’ll get to it in time.”

Time? What time???

Carlos spotted another dud and snipped it. They'd cleared a lot of wires, and it was getting clearer now. If they had just a few more minutes, they could do it.

But they didn’t have a few more minutes. They barely had …

He forced himself not to look. He forced himself to look at the wires. Oh, so many wires.

“Wait. What about this one?”

He pointed at a wire. It was tucked behind three unmarked and two marked wires.

Almost as if whoever planted this bomb wanted to hide it.

“Good eye, Carlos. Let’s take a look at the wires in front. Cut the left one. Good. Hmm, doesn’t give us a better view. Oh, good. Yeah, move it a bit more. Yes, cut the red one in back. Good job. Crouch down and look up. Yes, that’s it! Cut that wire.”

Carlos placed his wire cutters on the wire. “You sure?”

He couldn’t see how it connected the timer to the bomb.

“Yes, I’m sure.”

Carlos sure wasn’t sure. He glanced at the timer. Ten seconds. Someone put a hand on his shoulder and gave it a reassuring squeeze.

He took a deep breath and cut the wire.

Nothing happened. He didn't blow up, and the timer didn't stop.

“It’s not the right one!”

“It’s OK, Carlos. This type of timer keeps running after it’s defused.”

“You sure?”

“Yes.”

“But—”

The timer ran to zero and switched off. The bomb didn’t explode.

His friends cheered, but Carlos Pereira didn’t hear them. As soon as the clock switched off, he fainted and sank into his friends’ arms.

CHAPTER TWENTY SIX

Jacob sprinted downstairs in the dam near Bhaktapur, Nepal. It was the smallest dam of the ones targeted, but that didn't matter. It would still take out tens of thousands of people.

He ran with a couple of Nepali engineers as well as Jana and Bledshaw. That damn pilot took up the rear. Looked like he was going to be breathing down their necks for the rest of the mission.

Their mission might end pretty damn soon. The chief engineer, the only man who spoke decent English, had told him there were only minutes left to go on the timer.

They came to a hidden trapdoor that had been drilled and pried open by the Nepali engineers and was now flanked by several soldiers. They rushed down the stairs and came to a large room filled with antiquities. Jana let out a gasp of wonder at the sight of all the inscriptions and manuscripts. Even in a situation like this, she was still 100% the academic.

Jacob saw the line of drill holes topped with blasting caps, and the complex of cables that snaked to a mass of wires nearly covering a timer that was down to eight minutes.

He stood and stared. No way he could get through this mess in eight minutes.

Don't freeze. Oh, hell no. Not now.

He saw a camera in the upper corner of the room. Was the Curator watching? Was Professor Harlow?

"We have cut everything that we could see was a false wire," the chief engineer said.

Snipped wires littered the floor beneath the timer. Too few. Far, far too few.

Do. Not. Freeze.

Jacob forced himself into action. Giving the camera the finger, he strode over to the timer, picked up the wire cutters that lay on the floor beneath it, and got to work.

Everyone kept silent.

He breathed a little easier as he saw that this bomb was simpler than the others. A lot of the dud wires obviously didn't lead anywhere, and he snipped them away one by one in rapid succession.

Maybe this was going to be easy after all.

BANG!

The mass of wires blew out like a circle of little tentacles, and Jacob felt a hot impact in his midsection. He staggered back, clutching his stomach. Jana and Bledshaw caught him.

"What the hell?"

"A little bomb," the Nepali chief engineer said. "It looks like a small blasting cap hidden behind the wires. One of them was wired to it."

"Jesus," Jacob groaned. "One of the dud wires was actually a trap."

Pain radiated from his gut. He tore open his bloody shirt and saw the wound wasn't so bad—a nasty burn but the cut wasn't too deep. His hands were burned, too. A lucky thing he hadn't lost any fingers.

He checked the timer.

Six minutes.

"I'm OK. Got to get back to work."

He stood, wavered a moment, and walked back to the wires.

Now, he worked more carefully. Not only did he have to check if a wire led to the charges, he also had to make sure it didn't lead to a hidden blasting cap.

Luckily, the first blast had cleared a bunch of wires he could snip away. With some more probing, he found another hidden blasting cap, isolated it, and disarmed it.

His gut blazed with pain. He could feel a dampness running from his shirt to his pants. That wound was bleeding. It didn't matter. He wouldn't bleed to death in the time left on the bomb.

Jacob Snow's hands remained steady and his eyes clear as he worked to find more wires to cut.

After snipping a few more, he thought he had found the Holy Grail.

The wire that would defuse the bomb.

And he still had two minutes to go. Not too shabby.

Jacob checked and double checked. Yeah, it went to the timer.

He cut the wire.

BANG!

Jacob clutched his face, reeling back from the flare of light and the pain.

Another blasting cap? How?

Once again his companions caught him.

"Ugh, I can't see!"

His face felt like it was on fire. Powder burns. Dimly, he heard the sound of running feet.

"Here is some water from one of the soldier's canteens," the chief engineer said.

Someone poured water over his face. He sputtered and blinked and could finally see again. His eyes hurt and were probably redder than a hippie on the last day of Woodstock, but at least he could see.

Sort of. Things were a bit blurry. He squinted at the timer.

One minute.

He wiped his eyes, spat out some dust and a bit of blood, and got back to work.

No time to be careful. If something was absolutely, positively a trap, he left it. Otherwise, he cut it. He heard the chief engineer sucking the breath in between his teeth. As the only other person in the room who knew what he was doing, the poor man must have been having a heart attack to see Jacob throw caution to the wind.

It was that or let the dam burst.

Then he found it, at least he thought he did.

Was this the wire? It didn't look like a dud, and he had cleared enough wires to see there weren't any more blasting caps hidden behind them. Although that wasn't a guarantee. The one that blew in his face had been hidden in a recess in the wall and painted over. Sneaky little bastard.

He put the wire cutters over the wire he thought would defuse the bomb. He wiped his stinging eyes. One was swelling shut. The other was blurry. He squinted at the timer. Thirty seconds … twenty-nine seconds …

What if I'm wrong? I'll kill tens of thousands of people?

Even if it only sets off another blasting cap, I'll never recover in time to figure out the real wire.

Why can't I just be back at the cabin?

Twenty seconds.

Wait. What?

Jacob Snow had frozen again.

He felt a hand on his shoulder.

Jana.

"You can do this, Jacob. We all believe in you. I believe in you."

Jacob took a deep breath and cut the wire.

The readout winked out. The bomb was defused.

Jacob fell into Jana's arms in a loving embrace.

***

Watching Jacob defuse the bomb, Dr. Colin Harlow cursed and kicked the wall.

"Damn it! That was the last one!"

"You should have let me take care of them," said Agent Twelve, known to the police as Goran Hribar.

"Quiet!" Harlow snapped. "Let me think."

He paced back and forth as the men and women at the bank of computers didn't speak. They barely dared to breathe. Even Hribar, who could kill everyone in the room in less than a minute, kept quiet.

The man he knew as Agent Zero snapped his fingers.

"All is not lost. I've exposed the Antiquities Division and destroyed some of their best supporting evidence. The Curator will be in a much weaker position. His own men will be angry and discontented. And we've covered our tracks. They won't be able to find us."

Hribar wasn't so sure about that. What the Curator said next reassured them.

"We have a refuge in North Korea we can use. We'll go there. Even if they can find us, they can't chase us there, not while North Korea has nukes. Then we can plan our next move."

He turned to Goran Hribar.

"We have another way forward. It involves making allies with some people I trust even less than the North Koreans but who are far more powerful. They have their own agenda for world dominance. Perhaps we can combine forces."

Yes, the Order might just be the allies he needed.

The Curator smiled. "And you, Agent Twelve, will get your wish. Assemble a team of the best. Assassins and demolitions experts from among my personnel. You're going after these CIA agents and their archaeologist friend. Getting them out of the way will be our first step."

CHAPTER TWENTY SEVEN

Jana stood with Jacob and Bledshaw at the airport in Kathmandu. Jacob had been patched up by a Nepali army doctor, and even though he wore gauze over one eye and the other was red and puffy, there was no permanent damage. The pilot was ready to go, and a dozen men from the Antiquities Division had shown up in another plane and now stood nearby. Jana didn't need any specialized training to see they were all highly trained and dangerous.

Bledshaw managed a smile. It did not look convincing.

"Are you sure you want to go?" Jana asked. "We could protect you."

"The Curator won't harm me. I helped save the situation, after all."

"Well, I'd like you to call us," Jana said, raising her voice so the goons could hear. "Give us a call in a few days to let us know you're OK. And once a week after that."

"Yeah," Jacob said in a loud voice. "We're looking forward to hearing from you."

Bledshaw smiled. "I never thought seeing someone threatening my coworkers would feel so touching."

"They'll get some touching if they mess with you," Jacob said.

"I appreciate that. You know, I do believe our offer still stands. You certainly did far more than me to stop Professor Harlow. Why don't you join the Antiquities Division? This fight is far from over, and as a member of our organization, we could work much more closely."

"I already got a job," Jacob said. He looked at Jana, worry clouding his eyes.

"It's a tempting offer," Jana admitted, taking Jacob's hand. "But I don't think I like how your organization is run."

"That makes three of us," Bradshaw said. "Still, I have made my choice and I must help the Antiquities Division maintain its secrets. After what Professor Harlow did it's become all the more important."

"You think the U.S. government will even let you guys operate after what you pulled?" Jacob said. "And Harper Canyon was just the beginning. We got representatives from two dozen nations baying for your blood at the UN. I'm surprised they're even letting you leave the airport."

Bledshaw laughed. "Governments can't stop us, certainly not the U.S. government."

"The Turks lost 50,000 people. They've all but declared war on you."

"Food for the masses. They won't dare lift a finger."

Jana cocked her head. "Why not?"

Bledshaw shrugged. "Ancient secrets aren't our only specialty. We know quite a few modern ones too. No government of any importance dares touch us."

He extended a hand. Jana shook it.

"I'm not sure I like the implications of that statement," she said.

"Oh, we're not as sinister as all that. But all governments have secrets they need to hide, especially the democratic ones where the political parties have to put up a reasonable façade of caring for the people."

"Now, I really don't like the implications of what you're saying."

"Surely you couldn't have too many illusions left with Jacob Snow for a boyfriend." He turned and shook Jacob's hand. "I'm quite certain you don't have any left. Well, thank you ever so much for your help, and I'll make sure to call you on a regular basis. As soon as we find any leads in finding Professor Harlow, we'll share them all with you."

"You think the Curator will do that?"

"Oh, yes. He wants him dead. I think you can expect much better communication from now on."

"If we find any leads, we'll share them with you, like we're sharing intel with all other nations, enemy and ally. This is too big to get territorial."

"I think the Curator finally understands that. Good day."

With that, he turned and boarded the plane, followed by several of the Antiquities Division goons.

Jana watched him go.

"You know, Jacob, we've been on a lot of missions together, and it's been a hell of a ride. But this is the first time I'm left with absolutely no idea what's going on."

"It would look a lot clearer if you accepted their idea of an ancient supercivilization."

"That's ridiculous."

"Is it? They sure are fighting over something."

“Not that,” Jana said. “It has to be something else.”

“You sure?”

“Maybe. I don’t know. Jesus Christ, can we just go home now?”

“I thought you were getting bored at home.”

"I was," Jana said and sighed. "I am. After this, I need a break, just not a long one. I didn't like that our vacation was open-ended. It's like … I need this. We need this. We're so much more alive when we’re doing crazy stuff like this.” She turned to him. “Does that make sense? Does that make us insane or something?”

“Maybe. But looking back I realize that sitting around that cabin we were both sort of stagnating. It was pleasant, but I don’t think we’re cut out for that.”

Jana kissed him. “But we can enjoy it for a little while.”

Jacob returned her kissed and hugged her. “I have a feeling it really will only be for a little while. Hell, it might only be a day, so let’s enjoy it while we can.

NOW AVAILABLE!

TARGET NINE
(The Spy Game—Book #9)

"Thriller writing at its best... A gripping story that's hard to put down."
--Midwest Book Review, Diane Donovan (re *Any Means Necessary*)

From #1 bestselling and USA Today bestselling author Jack Mars, author of the critically acclaimed *Luke Stone* and *Agent Zero* series (with over 5,000 five-star reviews), comes an explosive new action-packed espionage series that takes readers on a wild ride across Europe, America, and the world—perfect for fans of Dan Brown, Daniel Silva and Jack Carr.

High up in the snowy mountains of Nepal, terrorists are on the verge of discovering one of the world's great archeological treasures and, crossing the border, threatening world security. Jacob must race to find them and stop them. But as he fights the world's harshest elements, Jacob soon realizes he may be walking right into a global trap….

An unputdownable action thriller with heart-pounding suspense and unforeseen twists, TARGET NINE is the ninth novel in an exhilarating new series by a #1 bestselling author that will make you fall in love with a brand-new action hero—and keep you turning pages late into the night.

Future books in the series will soon be available.

"One of the best thrillers I have read this year. The plot is intelligent and will keep you hooked from the beginning. The author did a superb job creating a set of characters who are fully developed and very much enjoyable. I can hardly wait for the sequel."
--Books and Movie Reviews, Roberto Mattos (re Any Means Necessary)

Jack Mars

Jack Mars is the USA Today bestselling author of the LUKE STONE thriller series, which includes seven books. He is also the author of the new FORGING OF LUKE STONE prequel series, comprising six books; of the AGENT ZERO spy thriller series, comprising twelve books; of the TROY STARK thriller series, comprising seven books; of the SPY GAME thriller series, comprising ten books; of the JAKE MERCER thriller series, comprising five books (and counting); and of the new TYLER WOLF thriller series, comprising five books (and counting).

Jack loves to hear from you, so please feel free to visit www.Jackmarsauthor.com to join the email list, receive a free book, receive free giveaways, connect on Facebook and Twitter, and stay in touch!

BOOKS BY JACK MARS

TYLER WOLF THRILLER SERIES
DOUBLE AGENT (Book #1)
DOUBLE CROSS (Book #2)
DOUBLE ASSET (Book #3)
DOUBLE DOCTRINE (Book #4)
DOUBLE JEOPARDY (Book #5)

JAKE MERCER THRILLER SERIES
ABSOLUTE THREAT (Book #1)
ABSOLUTE DAMAGE (Book #2)
ABSOLUTE FORCE (Book #3)
ABSOLUTE PERIL (Book #4)
ABSOLUTE TREASON (Book #5)

THE SPY GAME
TARGET ONE (Book #1)
TARGET TWO (Book #2)
TARGET THREE (Book #3)
TARGET FOUR (Book #4)
TARGET FIVE (Book #5)
TARGET SIX (Book #6)
TARGET SEVEN (Book #7)
TARGET EIGHT (Book #8)
TARGET NINE (Book #9)
TARGET TEN (Book #10)

TROY STARK THRILLER SERIES
ROGUE FORCE (Book #1)
ROGUE COMMAND (Book #2)
ROGUE TARGET (Book #3)
ROGUE MISSION (Book #4)
ROGUE SHOT (Book #5)
ROGUE STRIKE (Book #6)
ROGUE ORDER (Book #7)

LUKE STONE THRILLER SERIES

ANY MEANS NECESSARY (Book #1)
OATH OF OFFICE (Book #2)
SITUATION ROOM (Book #3)
OPPOSE ANY FOE (Book #4)
PRESIDENT ELECT (Book #5)
OUR SACRED HONOR (Book #6)
HOUSE DIVIDED (Book #7)

FORGING OF LUKE STONE PREQUEL SERIES

PRIMARY TARGET (Book #1)
PRIMARY COMMAND (Book #2)
PRIMARY THREAT (Book #3)
PRIMARY GLORY (Book #4)
PRIMARY VALOR (Book #5)
PRIMARY DUTY (Book #6)

AN AGENT ZERO SPY THRILLER SERIES

AGENT ZERO (Book #1)
TARGET ZERO (Book #2)
HUNTING ZERO (Book #3)
TRAPPING ZERO (Book #4)
FILE ZERO (Book #5)
RECALL ZERO (Book #6)
ASSASSIN ZERO (Book #7)
DECOY ZERO (Book #8)
CHASING ZERO (Book #9)
VENGEANCE ZERO (Book #10)
ZERO ZERO (Book #11)
ABSOLUTE ZERO (Book #12)

Made in the USA
Columbia, SC
26 September 2024